RED SLIDER

Jimmy,

Be a good friend!

Blair Hickson Riley

RED SLIDER

Blair Hickson Riley

Illustrations by Abby Crews

iUniverse, Inc.
New York Lincoln Shanghai

Red Slider

iUniverse books may be ordered through booksellers or by contacting:

iUniverse
2021 Pine Lake Road, Suite 100
Lincoln, NE 68512
www.iuniverse.com
1-800-Authors (1-800-288-4677)

This is a work of fiction. All of the characters, names, incidents, organizations and dialogue in this novel are either the products of the author's imagination or are used fictitiously.

ISBN-13: 978-0-595-39840-9 (pbk)
ISBN-13: 978-0-595-67748-1 (cloth)
ISBN-13: 978-0-595-84244-5 (ebk)
ISBN-10: 0-595-39840-5 (pbk)
ISBN-10: 0-595-67748-7 (cloth)
ISBN-10: 0-595-84244-5 (ebk)

Printed in the United States of America

For my mother, who would never leave a turtle on the road, and for her parents, Grandpa Jeremiah and Nana, who devoted much of their lives to nature education.

Contents

Acknowledgments

Special thanks are due to my family for their patience and encouragement, and to my wonderful, talented writing friends who provided feedback on *Red Slider*: Abby, Carol, Gloria, Ian, Judy, Lisa, Lori, and Sheela. I am also indebted to my writing teacher, the marvelous Jean Fritz, and my classmates Andrea, Cathy, Cynthia, Grace, Jeanette, Kristin, Linda, Liz, Rosemarie, and Selene.

Chapter 1

The Rumblers

The earth tossed and tumbled, shaking Benjamin and the other turtles from their log. A whirl of shells and claws tore through the water, fleeing from the horrible, unseen thing. Benjamin felt himself dragged downward, sucked into the whirlpool created by the rapidly escaping turtles.

"Rumblers!" yelled one turtle from below him.

"Got to be," shouted another, rushing into the murky depths of the pond.

Benjamin spun to a stop, abandoned by the quickly retreating turtles. Against his better judgment, he climbed back toward the sunlight. Poking his nose through the surface of the water, he breathed in, sniffing for any sign of danger. The air smelled different—earthier—but not terrible. He raised his head a bit more until his eyes were above the surface.

"What's up?" hollered Hopper, balanced on a nearby lily pad. Nothing ever rattled Hopper. He was the bravest animal Benjamin knew.

"I'm not sure," replied Benjamin. "I heard someone say it was rumblers."

Hopper bounced up and down on the lily pad. The frog's green skin shone in the morning sun as he said, "I can't think of anything else that would make that much noise. But I've never heard such loud rumblers before. Not ever."

The ground shook again, sending ripples across the surface of the pond. Hopper's lily pad trembled on its stalk.

"It doesn't sound like it's coming from Rumbler Run," said Benjamin, gesturing toward the hill bordering the east side of the pond. "It sounds like it's coming from across the Great Divide." Benjamin looked at the steep mound of soil rising toward the sky from the pond's south end.

Without thinking, Hopper stretched his powerful hind legs and sprang into the air. He landed gracefully on the shore and hopped to the south end. Benjamin dove under the water and swam to meet him. Just as they arrived, a deafening roar thundered across the pond. Dirt and mud flew through the air and splattered Hopper. Had the same thing happened to Benjamin, he would have been grateful, because instead of mud something large and heavy landed on him. Were Benjamin on land rather than in water, his shell would have certainly been damaged.

"Mmmph!" groaned Benjamin, suddenly underwater again.

The heavy object slid off to one side, and Benjamin scrambled back to the surface to check on Hopper. The small green frog seemed not to notice the mud, which had formed a little cap on his head. Instead he stared at the water next to Benjamin.

"Who's that?" he asked.

Benjamin wasn't aware that it was a "who" and not a "what" that had flown out of the air and pushed him under the water. But sure enough, a slightly dazed girl turtle floated to the pond's surface next to him.

"Where am I?" the turtle asked.

"You're on Earth," said Hopper. "Where did you come from? I've never seen turtles fall from the sky before."

"Well, I've never fallen from the sky before," she said. "I'm just not that sort of turtle."

"What sort of turtle are you?" asked Benjamin. "You don't look like a painted or a snapper." Benjamin studied the bright yellow spots on the new turtle's back.

"That's because I'm a spotted," she replied. "At least...I think I am."

"I've never heard of those before," said Benjamin.

"Well, I've never seen a turtle like you before, either," said the new turtle. "Of course, I'm a little dizzy right now, so maybe I have."

"I'm a slider," said Benjamin, a hint of sadness in his voice. "We're pretty rare around here."

"Not as rare as flying spotted turtles," said Hopper, trying to cheer up his friend. He turned to the spotted turtle. "You certainly are loud when you fly."

The spotted turtle huffed, "Well, I don't fly. I'm pretty sure about that. I just wish I could remember..." She stopped suddenly. Her jaw dropped, and she shook her head a single time, as though throwing off a buzzing fly.

"Wait!" she said. "I'm...I'm starting to remember some of it now." Her eyes grew wide with terror. "Rumblers. It was rumblers. There were two of them. The biggest rumblers I've ever seen. Oh my. Oh my."

"What is it?" asked Benjamin.

"My pond...they destroyed my pond!" The spotted turtle sobbed uncontrollably. "And everyone in it, I think. I'm the last one. Those horrible beasts must have thrown me over here."

Hopper shook his head sadly. "The sole survivor."

Benjamin tried his best to comfort the spotted turtle, but nothing he said helped. So Benjamin and Hopper just stood there, watching her cry.

As time passed, turtles slowly came out of the pond to crawl back onto their sunny logs. Two of the younger painted turtles swam over to the south shore to see what Benjamin was doing. One had a large dent in his dull shell; the other had a shiny shell, but a twisted smile.

"What's up, Slider?" asked the shiny turtle.

"My *name* is Benjamin," said Benjamin. He was sick of Gorn always calling him Slider.

"Whatever. So, what's going on, Bendy Man?" asked Gorn.

"This turtle fell from the sky and hit me," said Benjamin, ignoring Gorn's latest insult.

"A flying turtle?" asked the dented turtle.

"Of course not," snipped Hopper.

"You'd better get lost before I eat you," snapped Gorn, lunging toward the small frog.

Hopper darted away, but not without shaking the mud from his head onto Gorn's snout first.

Gorn sneered. "I swear, Slider. I don't know why you don't eat that thing."

"He's my friend," said Benjamin. Benjamin knew he was the only turtle with a frog for a friend. Turtles were supposed to eat frogs.

Gorn rolled his eyes and turned back to the spotted turtle. "And who exactly are you?"

The spotted turtle stopped sobbing long enough to answer. "My…my name is Dot."

The dented turtle burst into laughter. "A spotted turtle called Dot? That's a good one!"

"Knock it off, Kip," said Benjamin. "Can't you see she's really ups—"

Benjamin stopped suddenly and looked at Kip. "Wait a second," he said. "How did you know she was a spotted turtle?"

"Because I met some spotted turtles during my adventure," said Kip.

Everyone in Turtle Pond knew the story of Kip's adventure. Kip wasn't the smartest turtle in the pond; if he were, he would've known better than to try to cross Rumbler Run. Nobody ever crossed Rumbler Run unless they had to. Sure, the female snappers crossed the Run every year to lay their eggs, but they didn't want to do it— they had to do it. And many of them never got back. Why Kip had tried to cross the Run, nobody ever knew for sure; most turtles assumed Gorn had put him up to it. What everybody did know, though, was that a rumbler had gotten him.

As the story goes, Gorn and Prince Roux had been watching when Kip tried to get across. Unfortunately for Kip, turtles are among the slowest animals on land, and rumblers are the fastest. No sooner had he stepped onto the Run than a rumbler whizzed by, knocking him back toward the pond...only instead of sliding into the pond, Kip bounced twice and went straight over the Great Divide. Everyone was sure he was dead. It took him days to claw his way over the hill to get back home. When he emerged over the top of the Divide, he was like a ghost returning from the great beyond. The baby painters were scared to get near him for at least a month.

The rumbler must've banged up Kip's brain too, because he came back with the crazy idea that there was another pond just like theirs on the other side of the Divide. There were painters and snappers there, he said. Only there were polka-dot turtles too. Having never seen polka-dot turtles before, everyone assumed he was crazy.

Benjamin looked at Kip and gasped. "You really *did* see polka-dot turtles," he said.

Kip sighed. "Like I told you all before, there were spotted turtles over there."

Dot burst back into deep, heaving sobs. "And they're all gone! The rumblers ran right through the pond and destroyed it!"

As though the rumblers heard her, they suddenly came to life, growling and thundering against the other side of the Great Divide.

Large chunks of sod broke loose from the cliff and splashed into the pond. Benjamin and the others dodged the falling mounds of dirt and dove into the depths of the water.

"We've got to see the king about this," said Benjamin.

For the first time in his young turtle life, Gorn agreed with Benjamin, and the four turtles headed off toward the king's palace.

The palace was formed by two rotten logs under a weedy overhang along the pond's north shore. The floor of the king's home was thick with rich, dark glop. Tiny bubbles of algae foamed against the edges of the mud, creating a dense layer of pond scum. Overhead the weeds wove a tapestry of green, yellow, greenish yellow, and yellowish green. No place in Turtle Pond was grander.

King Titus sat with his belly nestled into the muddy bottom of the palace. Several of the more important painted turtles were gathered around him, apparently discussing the day's alarming events. Prince Roux leaned in close to the old king, whispering.

"King Titus! King Titus!" yelled Benjamin.

"Real dignified," sneered Gorn. Kip snickered.

Benjamin ignored them and approached the pond's leaders. The king lifted his royal head and studied Benjamin's face.

"Do you come with news, young slider?" the king asked.

Benjamin nudged Dot forward with his nose. "This is Dot. She's a spotted turtle from a pond across the Great Divide."

The entire committee of painted turtles turned and looked at Kip, as though to say, "Well, he's not crazy after all." This did not escape the attention of Kip, who instantly produced a self-satisfied smile.

They turned back to Dot. Some of the turtles moved toward her for a closer look. Others drew back, alarmed by her unusual appearance. Dot trembled, having never been in the presence of a king and his royal court before.

The king took a moment to gain his composure, then cleared his throat. "Tell me, young, uh, polka-dot turtle, what news do you bring?"

Dot sniffled, then started into her sad tale. The king listened carefully, nodding. Then he looked at the nervous young turtle with kind eyes.

"You may remain here with us. I hereby decree that you are to be accepted as one of our own…a true citizen of Turtle Pond."

Before Dot had a chance to thank King Titus for his generosity, two turtles scurried into the hollow, huffing and puffing. Their eyes darted back and forth, as though watching for a dreadful monster.

"Tulegs! There are tulegs by the pond!"

Chapter 2

The Tulegs

As terrible as the rumblers were, there was nothing the turtles feared more than tulegs. Rumblers were large and loud; they made the earth shudder and the pond shake. But tulegs were worse. They were cold, cruel, and calculating. While the rumblers just roared through everything, unseeing and unthinking, the tulegs planned and hunted. Their skin was smooth, their eyes large and probing. Tulegs were the most horrible creatures on earth. And wherever there were rumblers, there were tulegs. It was as though the tulegs held the rumblers under a spell, urging them on for their own purposes.

King Titus shifted uneasily, coaxing sucking sounds from the thick mud under his belly. "Tulegs? Are you sure?"

Prince Roux raised his noble head. "Where there are rumblers…"

Everyone knew what he was going to say. There was no need to finish. King Titus sucked in a great breath of air and let it out again. "Very well. Sentries! Go and report on the activities of the tulegs."

Two large painted turtles with bright red scallops edging their shells dove into the water. Benjamin leaned toward Dot. "Let's go," he whispered.

Dot's orange eyes widened with fear. "Is it safe?"

"Probably not," said Benjamin, "but we'll keep our distance."

With that Benjamin slid under the surface and swam toward a fallen log across the pond. Dot followed close behind. When they reached the log, they crawled to a hidden spot where the log met the shore. A small painted turtle was already wedged against the bank, studying the ground at the feet of the tulegs.

"Hi, Wibble," Benjamin whispered.

"Hey, Benjamin," said Wibble, his eyes unmoving.

"Careful," said Benjamin. "There are tulegs by the pond."

"I know," whispered Wibble. "That's why I'm here."

Benjamin looked at Wibble with disbelief. While Hopper was the most courageous animal he knew, Wibble was the least. Whenever a predator was near, Wibble was the first turtle to hide in the deep muck at the bottom of the pond. Even the sound of a duck quacking sent Wibble running, and ducks only attacked baby turtles. Benjamin couldn't believe Wibble would be so brave as to stay near the pond's surface when tulegs were around.

But Benjamin didn't need to wonder why Wibble was there for long. One of the tulegs dropped a shiny thing on the ground, and Wibble watched it with eager eyes. There was nothing Wibble loved more than tuleg shiners. The edges of his strange little den were stuffed with them—dozens of them. Most were silver, but some were glossy white, and others had strange tuleg symbols on them. Wibble, in fact, wore a soft tuleg shiner on his shell that very moment. It was anchored down with globs of sticky mud.

"Oh, brother," said Benjamin, looking from the shiner at the foot of the horrible tuleg to his friend's bright eyes.

While Wibble watched the shiner, Dot and Benjamin watched the tulegs. The tulegs wore shells on their heads and carried strange objects. The largest tuleg pointed at the pond and at the Great Divide, making complicated tuleg sounds. The other tulegs nodded, but Benjamin was certain they had no choice. After all, if tulegs were as cruel as everyone said, the biggest tuleg was surely a fearsome creature. Nobody would dare disobey.

After a period of pointing and murmuring, the tulegs climbed over the Great Divide and disappeared out of sight. In the distance, Benjamin saw a small, green object jumping along behind the large beasts. *Hopper*, he thought.

The moment the tulegs were gone, Wibble scurried over to retrieve the shiner. He slid back into the pond, grasping it tightly in his mouth. Dot and Benjamin started to follow him under the surface but were stopped by a small, yet forceful voice.

"Benjamin! Hey, Benjamin!"

Benjamin turned and found himself face to face with Hopper.

"I followed the tulegs," Hopper said. Dot looked at him hopefully.

"You were right, Dot. The rumblers destroyed whatever was over there. It's all just a big, soggy pile of dirt."

Dot's chin quivered, but she tried to be brave. Her bright orange eyes brimmed with tears.

Hopper bounced as he spoke. "The tulegs went over and sat right on top of the rumblers, forcing them to walk. They moved away from the Great Divide, but kept pointing at it. One tuleg kicked the cliff wall. I think they want it gone."

"We've got to tell the king!" said Benjamin for the second time that day. Hopper leaped into the water after Dot and Benjamin, but Benjamin blocked the way with his body.

"Not you, Hopper. To be perfectly honest, I'm afraid that some members of the court would...uh...eat you."

Hopper jumped onto a nearby lily pad and waved one front leg. "Well, if they did, I'd be sure to give them the worst stomachache they ever had!"

"Just the same," said Benjamin. "I'd hate to see you...well, you know."

"All right," said Hopper. "I'll stay here. But only because you asked me to. I'm not afraid of those guys."

"I know you're not," said Benjamin, and he meant it. Hopper waved one angry arm in the air while Benjamin and Dot swam off.

They arrived at the palace just as the sentries finished telling the king about the tulegs. Benjamin told the king everything Hopper had seen.

King Titus turned to his advisors. "What do you think of all this? Are we in danger? Will the tulegs make the rumblers attack?"

The advisors hemmed and hawed, as advisors will; nobody really wanted to take responsibility for a decision. Benjamin, who was normally a patient turtle, could see that the meeting was going nowhere.

He cleared his throat, so he could speak in his loudest voice. "Perhaps we should ask Jeremiah."

Everyone turned and stared at Benjamin. While the advisors knew Benjamin was probably right, asking Jeremiah seemed an even more unpleasant undertaking than making a decision themselves. After all, Jeremiah was very old and very, very grouchy. What's more, he occasionally ate young painters; snappers were known for that. But Jeremiah was the oldest turtle in the pond and had seen many times come and go, both good and bad. There was no doubt he would know best.

Benjamin stared at the unmoving turtles. Even Prince Roux, known as much for his courage as his pride, seemed unwilling to volunteer.

Benjamin fidgeted. Then he looked from Dot to the damaged wall of the Great Divide. For all they knew, the rumblers could return the very next day. Someone had to do something.

"I'll do it," said Benjamin. "Somebody's got to talk to him. I'll go visit the snapper."

Chapter 3

Jeremiah

Dot swam beside Benjamin. "Are you sure you want to go see Jeremiah?" she whispered. "Snappers are so grumpy."

Benjamin nodded. "He's been around for decades. He'll know what to do."

"Well, I'm going too," said Dot. "After all, I've got nothing to lose—"

"—except your life," said Benjamin.

Dot sighed. "My life was in the other pond. Everything I knew and loved was there until the rumblers came. I can't wait around for the same thing to happen here. I'm going with you."

Benjamin hated to put Dot in danger, but he was glad to have company. The closest he had ever come to Jeremiah was about ten steps away, and that was during a game of dare with the other young turtles. Almost every turtle in the pond had been within ten or fifteen steps of the old snapper on a dare—except Wibble, who hadn't even been within twenty. But Benjamin had never been close enough to Jeremiah to talk to him, and he wasn't looking forward to it.

The snappers in the pond kept to themselves. While the other turtles sat together on the logs, soaking in the sun's warmth, the snappers lurked in the depths. They were wily, stubborn, and unpredictable. Everyone feared them. It was no wonder, then, that Benjamin's heart pounded as he and Dot swam toward the deep muck at the bottom of the pond. Everyone knew that old turtles were grumpy, but an old snapper was downright dangerous, and Jeremiah was the oldest turtle in the pond.

Benjamin didn't see Jeremiah at first. His shell was so overgrown with algae that it looked like an ancient rock sitting on the bottom of the pond. If Jeremiah had been in a deep, murky spot, he would have been completely invisible. But unlike most snappers, Jeremiah chose to sit in a shallow part of the pond. The most stubborn sunbeams—those that snuck past the floating bits of algae and leaves—gave Benjamin the light he needed to see Jeremiah before he swam right over him.

Dot gasped. They had come up on the giant snapper suddenly. While she had heard about snappers this large, she had never seen one. They studied Jeremiah. He was at least ten times their size. His overgrown shell was thick and worn. Pieces of loose skin clung to the thick folds of his only exposed foot.

"He's monstrous," whispered Dot.

The thick mud beneath them shifted without warning. Powerful ripples spread upward from the spot.

"He's moving," said Dot, backing away.

"Shhh," warned Benjamin.

A huge head emerged from under the rough shell slowly and steadily, like a barge floating under a bridge. The snapper seemed unaware of the young turtles floating over him. After a leisurely stretch, he opened his large mouth.

"He's going to attack," shrieked Dot, backpaddling more rapidly now. The rear of her shell crashed into a sunken log. She darted behind Benjamin.

Benjamin tried to be brave but felt small and alone.

"Excuse me, Mr. Jeremiah, sir?"

The large snapper stopped stretching and poked his pointed snout back and forth, searching for the source of the voice. The snout came to a halt directly in front of Benjamin.

A low rumble issued from Jeremiah's throat. Benjamin trembled like a salamander facing a water snake. If snappers sometimes ate young painted turtles, didn't that mean they might eat sliders too? Was he small enough to eat?

"Who's there?" growled the snapper.

It took Benjamin a few seconds to gather the courage to speak. "It's, uh, Benjamin."

"What's a Benjamin?" asked Jeremiah in a gruff voice.

Benjamin swam a few inches closer to Jeremiah. "I'm Benjamin," he said. "I'm a young turtle from the pond."

Jeremiah squinted, trying to make him out through his old eyes. "Come closer," he demanded.

Benjamin swallowed hard. "You're not going to eat me, are you?"

A horrifying sound rang through the pond. Benjamin looked around, but the noise was definitely coming from Jeremiah. At first Benjamin thought the snapper was preparing to attack. Then he worried that Jeremiah was dying. Finally he realized that the ancient snapper was laughing. His laughter ended in a long, deep cough.

"Eat you?" Jeremiah sputtered. "I haven't eaten another turtle in at least a decade."

Benjamin sighed with relief. "Well, that's good."

Jeremiah narrowed his eyes. "But I've bitten plenty."

Benjamin froze. He could feel the water vibrating where Dot trembled behind him.

Jeremiah chuckled again. "Don't worry, I'm not in a biting mood today. Why have you come? You ought to know that snappers like to be left alone."

Benjamin gulped. "Well, sir, it's just that we need your advice."

"My advice? And what advice would that be, exactly?"

"Well, sir," said Benjamin, "there's been an attack on the pond across the Great Divide. It's been destroyed by rumblers."

Jeremiah's smirk dissolved into a serious expression. "Destroyed by rumblers?"

"Yes," said Benjamin quickly, encouraged by Jeremiah's concern. "We…that is, the king…was wondering if you thought they would come here too."

Jeremiah blinked his cloudy eyes. He lowered his voice. "Have the tulegs been by the pond?"

Benjamin's eyes widened. "Why, yes, they have."

Staring straight ahead, Jeremiah murmured, "The time has come."

"Excuse me, sir," said Benjamin. "What time?"

Jeremiah spoke in a quiet voice. "The prophecy."

"The prophecy?" echoed Benjamin.

Jeremiah shifted uneasily, and the pond quivered in his wake. "There's an old snapper prophecy, made long ago by turtles older and wiser than I."

Benjamin drew closer to hear the snapper's words.

"One day the tulegs will come. They will destroy Turtle Pond and everything in it. During these darkest of times, a new leader will rise from the midst. He will lead the turtles to a new land…a paradise."

"A paradise? But where?" asked Benjamin.

"A beautiful place. A wonderful pond, far from the rumblers and tulegs."

Benjamin imagined such a place: fresh, clean water, with sunny logs all around the sides. "But how will we find it?"

"I don't know," said Jeremiah. He leaned in closer. "But there have been tales of such a place. Sometimes a female snapper will tell of it after returning from laying her eggs. And the geese…they too speak of it."

Benjamin panicked. "But the female turtles cross Rumbler Run when they lay their eggs. We can't go there. We'll all be killed!"

"The new leader will bring you there safely. The prophecy says so," repeated Jeremiah.

"But who will this new leader be?" asked Benjamin.

Jeremiah shook his head slowly. "I don't know. There is only one thing the prophecy says about the new leader: he will be a Red."

Chapter 4

The Red

Everyone in Turtle Pond knew about Reds. The bellies of painted turtles were usually an orangish yellow or a yellowish orange—but much, much more rarely, they were a reddish yellowish orange. It was these painted turtles, with bellies like the setting autumn sun, who were called Reds.

"There are only three Reds in the pond," said King Titus after Benjamin and Dot returned with their news. But everyone knew which of the three was the prophesized leader.

Prince Roux stepped forward. His shiny shell sparkled. "I'm the prince, so naturally I should be the Red to do it."

King Titus beamed at Prince Roux. "And that is why I made you the prince." The king lifted his chin, addressing the others in a loud voice. "Confidence. Pride. Majesty. It is these traits that make a leader."

Benjamin looked at the young prince with admiration. Indeed Prince Roux was a handsome turtle, and he knew how to work a crowd. Standing on the soft, algae-laden log, Prince Roux lifted his eyes to the sky. Below his outstretched neck, his perfectly polished shell glimmered and shined. He was a sight to behold. Benjamin felt like cheering. *Yes, of course*, he thought. *Prince Roux will save us all!*

After a seemingly endless number of committee meetings, it was decided that Prince Roux should try to cross Rumbler Run after dark, when there were fewer rumblers. Because the destruction of their pond could happen any day, it was further decided that he should cross that very night.

Once the air grew cool in the face of the fading sun, and the crickets started their evening melody of chirps, the turtles gathered at the edge of Rumbler Run. Prince Roux stood in front of the others.

"He's not even nervous," whispered Benjamin to Wibble and Dot.

"He's a fool not to be," said Wibble, who trembled at the thought of crossing the rumbler run. The shiner he wore wrapped around his head rustled and crinkled, intruding upon the gentle sounds of the night.

Hopper peeked out from behind Dot. "Well, I'd do it. And I wouldn't be the least bit afraid."

"Of course you wouldn't," agreed Benjamin.

Dot shifted to hide Hopper. "But you *should* be afraid of getting eaten by one of the other turtles. Please stay hidden."

"I'm not afraid of them," said Hopper, but he sunk behind Dot anyway when Benjamin shot him a warning glance.

Prince Roux turned to the crowd. His voice was young and strong. "Fellow turtles, tonight I cross Rumbler Run to find us a new home." He looked toward the baby turtles. "Do not fear, little ones, for I shall save us all…just as the prophecy has foretold."

Prince Roux turned and walked slowly onto the Run. He walked slowly not because he was lazy, or frightened, or cautious. He walked slowly because he was a turtle, and that's what turtles do. Prince Roux couldn't have walked any faster, even with a large bear chasing him. Fortunately there weren't any bears out that night.

But there were rumblers.

Prince Roux wasn't even a quarter of the way across the Run when a rumbler appeared on the horizon, its bright, white eyes piercing the darkness, unseeing.

"Watch out!" shrieked Dot.

The other turtles hollered and shouted. They bobbed their heads up and down, filled with fear and dread.

For the first time in his picture-perfect life, Prince Roux trembled. He moved his stubby little turtle legs as quickly as he could to escape the rumbler.

"Run! Run!" shouted the other turtles.

But the whole scene took only seconds, for rumblers were as fast as turtles were slow, and Prince Roux had no hope of outrunning it.

RUMBLE! RUMBLE! WHOOSH!

The rumbler whipped by the turtles. Its roaring wind knocked the smaller turtles backward, and one tumbled down the hill and into Turtle Pond.

"Roux!" hollered King Titus, losing his kingly composure.

"Stay here, sire," said the captain of the guard. He and two of his soldiers moved toward the spot where Prince Roux had stood before the rumbler came.

"It's not a pretty sight!" yelled back the captain.

Benjamin hung his head, sure that Prince Roux had been squashed by the rumbler. They had seen it happen before.

Narrowing his eyes, he searched the darkness for any sign of movement. Soon a group of turtles emerged into the dim light of the half moon.

"Thank heavens!" yelled King Titus.

Indeed the figure of Prince Roux, fully intact, broke through the darkness into the light, riding atop the two soldiers. Everyone cheered to see their courageous prince in one piece. The rumbler's large feet had missed him completely.

The merriment was quickly replaced by somber silence when the soldiers came close enough for everyone to see Prince Roux's face. Benjamin's jaw dropped. Dot let a weak squeak escape from her throat. Wibble trembled so hard that the shiner on his head fell onto the gravel. Even Hopper, still crouched behind Dot, turned a paler shade of green.

It would have been terrible if Prince Roux the Magnificent had been squished by a rumbler. It was, however, even more terrible to see the pale, trembling face of the once-confident prince filled with terror. Prince Roux's eyes were wide, his gaze fixed forward. He was trapped in the grip of fear, and it would be many days before he was able to leave his favorite spot under the mossy log.

"Well, that's that," said Benjamin. "We're doomed."

Chapter 5

The Other Reds

A cloud of hopelessness covered Turtle Pond the following day. There were only three Reds in the pond, and Prince Roux had been the most courageous of them. Several of the turtles in the high court tended to Prince Roux, trying to get him to eat and drink, while the rest spent the day in committee meetings. Benjamin and Dot swam back and forth in front of the palace, waiting for a decision to be announced. Wibble was nowhere to be found.

The sun had begun its slow descent toward the mountains when the king finally came out of the meetings. The turtles all gathered to hear his announcement.

"The wise snappers of old prophesized that a Red would lead us to safety. As such, the remaining two Reds in the pond will have to try Rumbler Run."

Everyone in the pond turned to search for the other Reds. Their eyes immediately fell on Kip. Unlike Prince Roux, Kip was no majestic leader. Big and unrefined, he wore terrible scars from his first jaunt onto Rumbler Run. He blinked his dull eyes.

"All right, all right," he said. "It's not like I've never been on the Run before."

Gorn snickered by his side. "Yeah, but you were dared to that time…and it didn't go so well."

Kip sighed. "And this time I have no choice."

Benjamin's heart flooded with a new respect for Kip. As ordinary as Kip was, he stood there ready to fulfill his duty.

That night the turtles gathered again at the side of Rumbler Run. The mood was very different than the night before. There was no pageantry. No speeches. No assumption of success. No noble, courageous hero waiting at the side of the road, ready to save them all. Instead Kip stood there, battered, deformed, and dull. The other turtles fidgeted and chattered, unsure of what to expect.

"Go ahead," said King Titus. "We thank you for your sacrifice. May luck be with you."

He didn't say anything about courage or nobility, thought Benjamin. Looking at Kip's twisted form, he understood why. But somehow the lack of praise didn't seem right. Wasn't Kip taking just as much of a chance with his life as Prince Roux had the night before?

Unfortunately Kip's second walk across Rumbler Run didn't go much better than his first. He had made it almost halfway across the Run when a rumbler appeared.

"It's like they know when a turtle is there," whispered Dot when the bright eyes appeared on the horizon. Benjamin held his breath.

Kip didn't tremble. His eyes never grew wide with terror. Instead he looked steadily toward the opposite side of the Run, determined to do his best to get across. His short legs moved frantically, his movement single-minded.

The turtles heard the crash as the rumbler's wind blew into their faces.

"He's been hit!" yelled Dot.

"Duck!" shouted Hopper from behind Benjamin.

The turtles looked up and saw the battered form of Kip flying through the air toward them. Benjamin and Dot tried to get out of the way, but turtles flung by rumblers moved almost as quickly as rumblers themselves, and Kip landed squarely on Dot's back.

"Umph!" moaned Dot, collapsing onto the ground. Kip ricocheted off Dot and bounced down the hill, into Turtle Pond.

Benjamin turned and scrambled into the water. He searched in the murky darkness where he had seen Kip disappear. Turning this way and that, his short claws in front of him, he tried to find Kip's body. Just when he was ready to give up hope, his tail brushed against something hard. He swung around and pushed his nose against Kip's shell. Making his neck strong, he used his head to push Kip to the surface.

"There he is!" shouted King Titus.

Several of the royal guards swam over and took Kip. The rest came down the hill with Dot on their backs.

"Are they alive?" asked Benjamin.

"Yes, they are," said Medi, an old painted who tended to sick turtles. "Quick, bring them over to my mud pit."

"This is a disaster," said Benjamin. "This time, two turtles got hurt. How will we ever get to the new pond?"

King Titus's voice boomed across the pond. "It is time for the final Red to cross the Run."

Everyone looked back and forth, searching for the third Red.

"He's not here," sneered Gorn. "Typical. He's such a wimp."

"Is not," said Benjamin.

"Find him," boomed King Titus.

Benjamin dove into the depths of the pond.

"Wibble?" Benjamin whispered. "Are you there?"

"No," said Wibble.

"C'mon, Wibble. They're looking for you."

"I'm not coming out." Wibble's voice was firm.

Benjamin poked his head into Wibble's favorite spot under the bank's weedy overhang. "You've got to. It's the prophecy. You're the last Red."

Wibble's greenish black head appeared from under a soft bed of rotting leaves. "Am not."

Benjamin sighed. "You are. Everybody knows it."

"I'm not," insisted Wibble. "Prove it."

"We certainly will," said a loud voice from behind Benjamin. The captain of the guard appeared out of the murky water. "You will come with us."

"Fine," said Wibble.

Benjamin swam along behind Wibble and the guards until they reached the edge of the pond. Wibble climbed out of the water with his head high and his jaw set.

"Onto your back," demanded King Titus.

The other turtles gasped. Asking a turtle to lie on his or her back just wasn't done in polite society.

King Titus stared hard at his subjects. "I know these measures seem extreme, but this is an emergency. The prophecy says that a Red will save us, and Wibble here insists that we are mistaken about his…uh…Redness."

Wibble hesitated, torn between his strong desire to protect his pride and his stronger desire to protect himself from the rumblers. Finally he rolled over onto his back, causing the younger turtles to gasp.

Wibble's shell was not reddish yellowish orange. Nor was it yellowish orange or orangish yellow. Instead it was shiny silver and pale purple and bright blue. It had strange symbols and lines all over it.

"Tuleg symbols," whispered one of the guards.

Benjamin hung his head. Wibble had used mud to stick dozens of shiners to his belly. They completely covered his real shell.

King Titus remained determined. "Remove those things."

"Gladly," said the captain of the guard, moving toward Wibble with his jaw open and his sharp claws ready.

Wibble wiggled his stubby legs. "No! No! You'll tear them. Don't!" He tried to turn himself over so that he could dive into the pond, but it was no use. Turtles stuck on their backs were sad, desperate sights—and never had there been a more pathetic display than this. Wibble cried and struggled and whimpered.

The guards tore the shiners off, ripping them to shreds. They took off one colorful strip at a time, until there was nothing there but a bright reddish yellowish orange shell peeking through streaks of thick mud.

"A Red," proclaimed King Titus. "To Rumbler Run."

The guards turned Wibble back over onto his belly. He nuzzled the ripped shiners with his snout, salty tears running into his mouth.

"You ruined my shiners! Just look at them!"

Benjamin stood alongside his friend and whispered into his ear. "Your torn shiners are the least of your problems, Wibble. You've got to cross Rumbler Run."

Wibble seemed not to hear Benjamin. He turned to the guards. "At least let me put them back first."

Normally the guards would have refused, but Wibble was such a sight with his watery eyes and runny nose that they felt sorry for him. How could they let him cross Rumbler Run in such a state? He would fail for sure, and then they would all die at the hands of the enormous rumblers.

"Very well," said the captain of the guard. "You may go and put away your things. But then you must meet us at the edge of Rumbler Run."

"Of course," said Wibble, sniffling.

He scooped up the torn shiners in his mouth and slowly headed back to his favorite spot under the weeds.

"I'll go with you," said Benjamin.

Wibble turned and smiled at his friend the best he could with a mouth full of shiners.

"Fanks, Benjhamin, bud I wand do be alone," he muttered.

Benjamin nodded. Wibble loved his shiners and wanted a private moment to put them away. Benjamin could understand that.

Just before diving into the water, Wibble looked back at Benjamin.

"Youw a good fwiend, Benjhamin," he said.

"You're a good friend too," said Benjamin. "I'll meet you by Rumbler Run."

The turtles waited by Rumbler Run for Wibble to appear. The air was crisp, and the moon was high in the sky. The sharp pebbles alongside Rumbler Run felt hard against their feet. Hopper bounced around behind Benjamin, impatient for the next attempt to begin.

"Stop it," warned Benjamin. "One of the other turtles is going to see you."

"What's taking him so long?" asked Hopper. "I mean, how long can it take to put away a few tuleg shiners?"

"He's upset," said Benjamin. "Give him some time to pull himself together."

Soon the evening chirps of the crickets gave way to late-night sounds. A lone owl hooted in a nearby tree and, deep in the woods, twigs cracked under the feet of late-night predators.

King Titus turned to his guards. "Bring him here now."

While Benjamin felt sorry for Wibble, he was relieved it would be over soon. His stomach ached with worry. What if Wibble got squashed?

The guards soon returned, panting.

The head guard took a deep breath. "He's gone."

"What do you mean, he's gone?" asked King Titus.

"I mean he's gone. He's not in his den. He's not anywhere in the pond. He's just gone."

"He ran away—the coward!" shouted Gorn.

Behind Benjamin, Hopper jumped back and forth, mumbling. "He ran away. He ran away. How could he do that?"

Benjamin was disappointed, but his disappointment quickly turned to dread. His best friend was alone somewhere in the night forest. What if a predator got Wibble? What if he couldn't find water or shelter? He could die.

"I've got to find him!" Benjamin said.

Hopper bolted out and stood in front of Benjamin. "You, find him? Turtles are too slow. You'll never catch up to him!"

Benjamin held his head high. "Well, I've got to try!"

Gorn's voice cut through the air. "Look! It's that frog. I think I'm hungry."

"Go, Hopper. Quick," said Benjamin.

Hopper darted away, but not without yelling back to his friend. "You stay here and look after Dot. I'll find Wibble. Don't worry about a thing!"

Benjamin smiled. Hopper was quick and smart. If anyone could find Wibble, Hopper could. Benjamin turned back to the other turtles, and his smile faded. Their faces hung heavy with despair. He could feel hope draining from the world of Turtle Pond. The prophecy said that a Red would lead them from danger, and they were out of Reds. Turtle Pond was in real trouble.

Chapter 6

Red is Red

So thick with despair was the pond the following morning that Benjamin could barely split the water with his claws. With all three Reds gone or injured, what would become of their world? Would they survive? What could they do to save themselves? Maybe Jeremiah would know.

Benjamin dove through the murky water, following the route to Jeremiah's favorite spot in the thick muck at the bottom of the pond. This time Benjamin felt no fear as he approached the old snapper's home.

"Jeremiah," he whispered, as though he carried the burden of a dreadful secret.

At first there was no response. Then he heard a low rumbling. Ripples of displaced water washed over him. Following the source of the ripples, he found Jeremiah.

"Is that you, young slider?"

"Yes," replied Benjamin. "I need your help."

The water vibrated with Jeremiah's throaty laughter. "Me? Now, how can I possibly help you?"

"You helped me last time," said Benjamin. "You told me about the prophecy."

"Ah, yes, that," said Jeremiah. Great sucking sounds came from the thick mud at the bottom of the pond as the snapper shifted his considerable weight. "How is that going?"

"Terribly," said Benjamin. "There were only three Reds in the pond. Two are hurt real bad, and the third has run away."

Benjamin was now close enough to see Jeremiah's face in the dim light of the pond. His eyes were calm and wise—a stark contrast with the gruffness of his voice. He studied Benjamin's face before speaking.

"Well, then," he said. "I suppose the task of leading the others to safety will fall on another."

"But what about the prophecy?" asked Benjamin.

Jeremiah produced a deep chuckle. "Yes, well, I imagine the leader *is* supposed to be a Red. But what is a Red?"

Benjamin rolled his eyes. "A turtle with a red belly, of course."

"Anything else?" Jeremiah stared at Benjamin with such intensity that the young slider looked away.

"No," said Benjamin. "That's what a Red is."

Jeremiah released his stare, and Benjamin looked at the snapper again. His eyes danced with mischief. If not for the gray wrinkles of Jeremiah's old neck, Benjamin would swear the snapper was a young turtle ready for a prank.

"What is red? Red is the color of the puffy flowers that bloom along the west shore when it gets warm. It's the color of the leaves on the tall trees when the winds come each fall. The plump berries on the north shore bushes shine a smooth, sleek red. Isn't it possible that the snappers of old had another meaning for the word red other than the bellies of the painted turtles?" asked Jeremiah. "Red is red."

Benjamin thought real hard, but the ideas swimming around in his head stayed just out of reach.

Jeremiah looked down casually, digging deep grooves in the thick mud with his claws. He changed the subject. "You don't look like the other turtles in the pond. I'm curious…what sort of turtle are you, Benjamin?"

"I'm a red-eared slider," said Benjamin, relieved at the break in tension, but saddened by the state of Jeremiah's aging memory.

"Pardon me?" asked Jeremiah. "I'm a little hard of hearing."

Benjamin moved closer to the old snapper and yelled, "I'M A RED…"

He stopped, and then quietly finished, "…eared slider."

Jeremiah smiled.

"Did I hear you say *red*?"

Benjamin didn't answer. He was lost in his own thoughts. Was *he* a Red? The painted turtles called those turtles with reddish bellies "Reds," but was that the only thing meant by "a Red"? What if Red *was* red? Anyone red. In any way.

Benjamin turned back to Jeremiah, who was waiting patiently.

"Are you saying that I'm a Red?" he asked.

"I'm saying that you are a *red*-eared slider. Who knows what the prophecy really means?"

"But I'm just an ordinary turtle. I'm not noble like Prince Roux. I'm not tough like Kip."

"And your friend Wibble?" asked Jeremiah, who somehow seemed to know about everything that went on in the pond.

Benjamin had to admit Wibble wasn't any great leader. He was scared of his own reflection.

Jeremiah's eyes twinkled. "Heroes don't have to be magnificent or tough. They don't need to be large or shiny. Heroes are ordinary turtles with the courage to rise to the occasion. The question you need to ask yourself, young Benjamin, is, do you have the courage?"

Chapter 7

An Ordinary Turtle

"You don't really expect a slider to lead us out of here, do you?" Gorn asked no one in particular.

Benjamin tried to ignore him. After all, Gorn wasn't standing at the edge of Rumbler Run, facing the possibility of a horrible, squishy death.

Gorn persisted. "Hey, Slider, why don't you slllllide across the Run?" Normally Gorn shared a good laugh with Kip whenever he said something that struck him as clever. But tonight Kip lay injured, and Gorn was forced to stand alone, scowling.

Ignore him, thought Benjamin. *Focus on the Run.*

He didn't have to ignore Gorn much longer. King Titus stepped to the front of the group for the third night in a row. "Silence!" Nobody needed to be told twice. After the events of the previous two evenings, the turtles took the Run very seriously.

"Benjamin, the red-eared slider, has volunteered to try Rumbler Run. I expect you all"—he paused and shot a threatening glance at Gorn—"to show some respect."

"But he's not a Red!" shouted one turtle.

"What about the prophecy?" asked another.

King Titus spoke in a loud, steady voice. "Young Benjamin is a red-eared slider. Perhaps that is red enough."

Benjamin faced Rumbler Run. Slowly he moved one claw onto its surface, preparing for the inevitable moment when he would try to scramble across. The gray surface of the Run was cold and hard. *Just like the rumblers*, Benjamin thought. *Cold and hard.*

"Whenever you're ready," said King Titus.

That was that. It was time to go. There would be no grand speeches, no noble ceremonies. Just him and the Run.

Benjamin looked to the right. No rumblers. He looked to the left. No rumblers. He took a deep breath and moved onto the Run. Hoping he wouldn't end up like Prince Roux or Kip, he walked quickly. Kip had gotten farther than Prince Roux, and he had moved steadily, always looking straight ahead. *Just keep walking*, Benjamin thought. *Straight ahead. Always straight ahead.*

But while his eyes never left the opposite side of the Run, his thoughts scurried all over. What if he didn't make it? Would it hurt to be hit by a rumbler? And what if he did make it? How would he ever get everyone else across? There were dozens of turtles.

He was halfway across, about where Kip had met his rumbler. *Halfway there.* Benjamin concentrated on the movement of his legs. *Faster. Faster.* The gravel on the other side of the Run drew closer. If only he could make it.

Like a ray of sun breaking through thick thunderclouds, a strong light penetrated the darkness of the night. Benjamin knew what that light meant: there was a rumbler coming. Behind him he heard the other turtles. Some shrieked. Others chattered. Many yelled, "Run! Run!" Just last night, Benjamin himself had shouted warnings to Kip.

He hastened his pace. The *scratch, scratch* of his claws against the hard surface of the Run quickened. Under him the ground vibrated and grumbled. The light grew brighter, forcing him to squint. He couldn't see, but he didn't need to. He knew where to go.

No longer did any of the turtles yell for him to run. The night air was alive with shrieks and gasps. A deafening roar filled Benjamin's ears, and the whole world flooded with a light so bright that the sun itself wouldn't have been able to compete. Benjamin didn't turn to look at the rumbler. Like Kip, he kept his attention focused on the other side. He didn't know how close the rumbler was until he heard a great screeching sound. It was the most terrible sound he had ever heard, worse even than the sound of a rabbit trapped in the jaws of a fox.

And then he felt the impact. It hurt, but not as much as he expected. What hurt more was the rolling over, and over, and over again that followed the crash. At the end of the long tumble, he lay still, suffocated by a strong odor in the air. There he was, a turtle on his back. There was nothing in the world more humiliating for a turtle than being stuck on his back, his stubby legs forced to wiggle and waggle in the air.

But Benjamin didn't wiggle his legs. Instead he looked around, trying to get his bearings. What he saw terrified him. Usually rumblers ran right down the Run, cold and uncaring. They never took any notice of the unfortunate turtles or frogs or raccoons that crossed their paths. But this rumbler stopped. There it stood, less than twenty steps from Benjamin, looking down at him with its bright, unfeeling eyes. For the first time since he had started across the Run, Benjamin was truly afraid. It was bad enough that the rumbler had hit him, but now it stood like a bobcat in front of a plump mouse, staring at its prey. What would it do? Did it plan to finish him off?

But soon Benjamin longed for the moment when only the great rumbler stood in front of him. For the only creatures on earth more terrible than rumblers were the clever, evil tulegs. Mere seconds after the rumbler stopped in front of Benjamin, the bright lights of the rumbler's eyes were blocked by a tall, frightening shadow. The shadow moved slowly toward him, its long arms and legs stretched forward. As it approached, Benjamin's heart filled with terror.

The tuleg reached its hot, spidery fingers toward him. Benjamin closed his eyes.

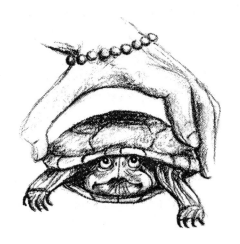

Chapter 8

The Red Tuleg

Benjamin trembled. Trapped on his back, he couldn't escape the tuleg. What would its terrible claws feel like? Would they be razor sharp? Hard and rough? He could feel the hot breath of the tuleg warming the night air. It drew closer. Then it grabbed him.

He opened his eyes. The hands of the tuleg weren't sharp or rough. They were soft and warm, like the moss on his favorite log after hours of bright sunshine. From the tuleg's mouth came sounds—high, soothing sounds, like the coos of a mourning dove. It looked at him with its eyes. Unlike the large, harsh eyes of the rumbler, the tuleg had small, gentle eyes. It wrapped its long arms around his body and held him close. Its warmth felt good through his scratched-up shell. All the while, it cooed and whispered.

The tuleg stood up and moved back toward the rumbler. Benjamin knew that wherever there were rumblers, there might be tulegs. The rumblers never hurt the tulegs, and only moved when tulegs commanded them to. But what Benjamin never realized before was that the tulegs rode inside the rumblers. He shuddered as the tuleg opened the belly of the rumbler and sat down within its great body.

Benjamin knew he should be terrified to be inside a rumbler. But the tuleg clicked gently like a cricket and stroked him with a soft hand. It didn't seem to want to hurt him. Though his heart pounded, he tried to remain calm. After all, he was alive, and the tuleg hadn't eaten him. The belly of the rumbler closed, trapping them within its cold, hard shell. He heard a great growling, and then the rumbler took off once more along the Run. Benjamin pulled his head and legs into the safety of his shell.

He stayed inside his shell for quite some time, vibrating in painful rhythm with the rumbler. All the while, the tuleg stroked him. At last the rumbler stopped, and Benjamin peeked out, just a bit, to see where they were. The tuleg opened the shell of the rumbler, and the rumbler's belly grew bright. Benjamin was surprised to see that there were two other tulegs in the rumbler. They were much larger than Benjamin's tuleg and spoke in deeper voices. He hadn't noticed them before, because they sat farther up in the belly of the rumbler.

Benjamin's tuleg climbed out of the rumbler, hugging Benjamin close to its warm body. In front of them was an enormous structure, rising to the sky like a small mountain. The taller tulegs walked toward it. Could it be their den? What would they do to him once they got inside? Benjamin withdrew into his shell again. He wasn't sure he wanted to find out.

The inside of the tuleg den was filled with a sweet smell—like flowers, but thicker. In the spring, the scent of fresh blossoms hung on the morning breeze, fluctuating around Turtle Pond. The odor in the tuleg's den was unwavering. Like a dense fog, it sat heavily in the air.

Benjamin dared once more to poke his head out. His eyes were assaulted by bright lights. Though it was no brighter than a sunny day at the pond, the den was too bright for nighttime. It was very large and filled with strange-looking objects in every color he had ever seen—and some he hadn't. The two large tulegs approached, and Benjamin pulled his head toward his bruised body. As though expecting Benjamin to be taken away, the smaller tuleg hugged him closer. Benjamin cringed, sore from the additional pressure. The large tulegs made strange sounds, and the smaller tuleg answered. The big tulegs showed their teeth. Their bright eyes shined. Were they preparing to eat him?

The smaller tuleg loosened its grip and turned Benjamin so that his belly was against its body. It looked down at him, and he looked up at its face. Above its gentle eyes, which were as green as Hopper's shiny skin, was a long mane of red fur. They had something in common, Benjamin and this creature. This tuleg was a Red.

Suddenly the Red tuleg took off running toward a tall hill made from smooth layers of rocks. It ascended the hill easily, as each rock was just the right size for its feet. The up-and-down motion of the climb intensified the pain in Benjamin's body. He clenched his jaw at each jolt, trying to ignore the deep ache radiating from inside his shell. The tuleg raced around a corner and into another room of the den. While this room also smelled sweet, its sweetness intermingled with another scent—a more familiar scent, like that of the pond. The room was the same bluish purple as wild asters in the fall. Tiny flowers decorated the walls and floor.

The tuleg turned, and Benjamin gasped. An entire wall of the purple room was covered with clear, water-filled dens: big dens and little dens, full dens and shallow dens. And in some of dens were turtles. He wondered why the tulegs had turtles in their home. Were they prisoners? Was this a storage area for turtles before they were eaten? Benjamin stuck his head out a little farther to get a better look. The small tuleg cooed and clucked when it saw his head out.

The tuleg carried Benjamin across the room and placed him in a big den with shallow water and a large rock. Benjamin quickly dove under the water, although it barely covered his shell. He crawled to a far corner of the enclosure and hid there. Luckily the tuleg didn't try to grab him back. Instead it busied itself picking up various items in the room. Some looked like tiny tulegs, except they were still and lifeless. Others looked like animals, plump and fuzzy, yet unmoving.

Benjamin sat for a while, watching the Red tuleg through the clear wall of his enclosure. It spun and skipped and moved around, its red fur bouncing this way and that. Sometimes it made high-pitched shrieks that somehow sounded happy, not frightened.

At last the tuleg tired and sat down on the floor of the room, surrounded by the strange objects. The two larger tulegs came in, and Benjamin saw that the tallest one had short, red fur. *It's a Red too*, he thought, feeling an unexpected kinship with the Red tulegs. After all, red was red.

Soon the large tulegs put Benjamin's tuleg into a soft nest, and the brightness of the room gave way to the darkness of night. The room grew silent, except for the steady rhythm of the tuleg's breath. Then a soft, high-pitched voice floated through the air like the gentle buzz of a hummingbird's wings.

"Are you a slider?"

Chapter 9

Cleo

"Who's there?" asked Benjamin.

"Cleo," said the soft voice.

"What are you?" he asked.

"I'm a slider. Are you a slider?"

Benjamin felt a rush of warm feelings. Another slider? Benjamin was the only slider in Turtle Pond. He had never met another slider before. He scrambled toward the voice. "Yes. Yes, I'm a slider," he said.

"Are you from the indoors or the outdoors?" asked the voice.

Benjamin kept searching in the dark. "What do you mean?" he asked.

"I mean, have you always lived with tulegs, or are you from a pond?"

Benjamin was shocked. Did turtles live with tulegs? He had never heard of such a thing before.

"I'm from a pond. Turtle Pond." Benjamin climbed up onto the rock to get a better view and found himself face to face with a small girl slider. A clear wall separated them, but her face was illuminated by a tiny star in the corner of the tuleg's room.

Cleo's eyes shone with curiosity. "Really? What's it like?"

Benjamin smiled. "It's beautiful. The edges of the pond are lined with rotting logs and thick mud. The water is deep and murky. In the summer, flowers and lily pads spring up all along the shore."

"Wow," said Cleo. "Sounds nice. It's nice here, too. Emlee feeds us yummy flakes every morning. Once a week, she changes the water in our tanks so that they're fresh and clean. During the day, she turns on our special lights to warm our rocks."

Benjamin looked up and saw the faint outline of a silvery object above him. "What's your name?" Cleo asked.

"Benjamin," he said.

"That's a strange name," said Cleo.

"I suppose it is," agreed Benjamin. "But I like it."

Cleo smiled. "I like it too."

"Thank you," said Benjamin. "I was wondering…do you think Emlee is a young tuleg? She seems small compared to the others."

Cleo's eyes flooded with love. "Yes, of course. She's a child. When she first got me, she could barely even climb the stairs herself."

"Stairs?" asked Benjamin.

Cleo giggled. "Yes, silly. You must have come up the stairs to get to Emlee's room. It's like a hill."

"Ah, yes," said Benjamin, remembering the painful jarring that accompanied the trip up the *stairs*.

Benjamin and Cleo spent the rest of the night with their faces pressed against the cool walls of their tanks. They traded stories about life with the tulegs and in Turtle Pond. By morning they were fast friends. Benjamin felt a lot better about being in the tuleg den. If Cleo liked it there, it couldn't be too horrible. And she really seemed fond of the Red tuleg child called Emlee.

After many hours, the dim glow of the moon gave way to the soft, pink rays of the morning sun. The room brightened, and Benjamin looked toward Emlee's nest. He knew a lot more about the little tuleg now, thanks to Cleo. He knew she was a girl. He knew she was kind and cared for the turtles in the tanks. Most important of all, he knew she didn't plan to eat him.

Emlee lay curled up in a ball under the soft covers of her nest, with nothing peeking out except her small nose and a few bits of her bright red fur. Benjamin decided then and there to trust the Red tuleg.

But he also decided he couldn't stay with her. He had to find a way back to the others in Turtle Pond.

He was their last hope.

Chapter 10

The Vet

When Emlee awoke, she sprinkled flakes into the turtles' tanks and turned on their lights, just as Cleo had said she would. Benjamin stared at the dry flakes floating on the surface of his still water. He turned to Cleo.

"Are you sure these things are good?" He wished he had some juicy pond plants.

Cleo played in her flakes, scooping them up in her mouth as she darted through them. "Sure, they're great!"

Benjamin reluctantly sank his mouth halfway into the water and scooped up a single flake. He swallowed the flake and the water. It felt dry against his tongue, but it wasn't as horrible as he had imagined. He ate some more, making a game of catching as many as he could in one mouthful. Once the last few flakes had made their way down his throat, he climbed onto the flat, gray rock in his tank. Its edge was sharp against his bruised body—not at all like the soft, algae-covered rocks of the pond. Still, the warmth of the light felt good. Cleo sat on her rock too. Together they warmed their bodies, aiding the digestion of their food.

"Maybe Emlee will bring us out of our tanks today," said Cleo. "Sometimes she lets us play outside."

Benjamin's mind raced. If he could get outside, maybe he could find his way back to Turtle Pond. He had to get back. The fate of the other turtles depended on it.

As though she had read Cleo's mind, Emlee appeared moments later, grasping a small enclosure. She reached into Benjamin's tank and wrapped her soft fingers around the edges of his shell. *She's bringing me outside*, he thought. *Maybe I can find a way home.*

"We're going outside!" Benjamin shouted. Cleo's eyes widened, and she shook her small head. The bright red stripes behind her eyes flicked back and forth, forming a blurry red band in the air.

Benjamin frowned, trying to figure out why she looked so worried.

Cleo dove off her rock and swam to the edge of her tank. She strained her lungs to make the most sound she could.

"The vet!" she yelled.

"The what?" shouted Benjamin with such force that he reawakened the deep ache from the rumbler crash.

"You're going to the vet!"

Cleo stared at the enclosure, and Benjamin followed her eyes. The vet seemed to be trouble, but he had no idea why; in fact, he had no clue what the vet was. Whatever it was, Cleo didn't seem too happy about it. In spite of his tender insides, Benjamin wiggled his legs. If the vet was a dangerous place, he would have to escape.

Try as he might, Benjamin couldn't get Emlee to loosen her grip. His short legs and claws landed far from the center of his shell, where her warm fingers still clutched him. No matter how far he stretched his neck, her hands were out of reach. He was trapped.

Ten minutes later, Benjamin found himself jiggling to and fro in the enclosure. The enclosure sat on Emlee's lap, and Emlee sat inside the rumbler. The tall Red tuleg was in the rumbler too, but farther up in its belly. Benjamin could hear its strange language and make out the top of its furry red head. The bouncing of the rumbler hurt Benjamin's sore body. Despite his best efforts, he was on the way to the vet.

The vet turned out to be more of an interesting place than a scary place, leading Benjamin to wonder why Cleo had been so upset by the thought of it. There were tulegs at the vet, but there were also a lot of other animals. Some of the animals trembled and moaned with fear and dread. One small, strange-looking bobcat wailed and hissed the whole time. Other small bobcats sat all over the room, and most were either sulking or clawing at things. Unlike bobcats in the forest near the pond, these came in a variety of colors: orange, black, white, gray, and brilliant mixtures of colors.

There were also wolf-like animals at the vet. These creatures barked and panted, jumping around their tulegs. Unlike the bobcats, the wolves seemed positively overjoyed to be at the vet. Like the bobcats, they came in all different colors—but they also came in many sizes. From the tiny white one yipping in the corner to the enormous yellow one lying across the feet of its tuleg, these wolves were happy.

Next to Emlee, a large tuleg with silver fur clutched a very big rat. The rat had long fur covering both its body and its face. When it spoke, it started every sentence with a great vibration.

"Wha-wha-what is wrong with you?" it said to Benjamin.

"Pardon me?" asked Benjamin.

"I-I-I-I-I said wha-wha-what is wrong with you?" said the furry rat once more, peering through a long lock of fur.

It hadn't occurred to Benjamin before, but perhaps his shell had been badly damaged by the rumbler. He wondered if his appearance was twisted and deformed, like Kip.

"I was hit by a rumbler," said Benjamin.

The large rat gasped, as did several wolves and bobcats who overheard. They all spoke at once.

"A rumbler?" "And you survived?" "How did it feel?" "Was it going fast?"

Benjamin wrinkled his forehead. He had never thought of an encounter with a rumbler as something to brag about. The other animals appeared awed by his experience.

"Yes, a rumbler," repeated Benjamin. "And it wasn't much fun, I can tell you that."

A small bobcat winced, and Benjamin quickly added, "But it was slowing down when it hit me. It didn't hit that hard."

The tiny bobcat released a long breath. The chatty rat clicked its tongue. "Weh-weh-well, that's certainly a good reason to go to the vet. Myself, I have a rather large tangle of hair stuck in my throat. Very uncomfortable business, that."

Benjamin studied the rat's long fur. He imagined a big ball of the stuff lodged in his own throat. Swallowing hard, he looked back at the poor animal.

"That sounds terrible," he said.

Benjamin supposed it might not be good manners to ask, but he wanted to know more about the hairy creature. "Excuse me, but what sort of rat are you?"

The creature pulled back, its mouth puckered indignantly. "A-a-a rat? How dare you! I'm no rat. I'm a gu-gu-guinea pig."

Benjamin looked down at his feet. "Oh, dear, I'm sorry. I didn't mean to upset you. I've never seen a guinea pig before. The closest thing I've ever seen is a rat."

The guinea pig relaxed its pursed lips. "Weh-weh-well then, no harm done. We're far more refined than rats. Where are you from that you've seen more rats than guinea pigs?"

Benjamin smiled, imagining his sunny log. "Turtle Pond," he replied.

The other animals stared at Benjamin, tittering and gossiping. "He's an outdoors animal," they said. "From the wild."

Benjamin remembered what Cleo had said about indoors animals and outdoors animals. "Do you live with tulegs?" he asked the others.

As though answering his question, the other animals snuggled deeply into their tulegs. The guinea pig wiggled its butt into the silver-furred tuleg's arm.

"Uh-uh-of course," he replied. "We're all pets. It's not often we see a wild animal at the vet."

Benjamin thought hard. Every animal in the room was with a tuleg. Like Cleo, they were fond of their tulegs. More surprising, the tulegs seemed fond of them. Some scratched their wolves' ears. One stroked the back of its bobcat. The bobcat made a soft, pleasant sound. Benjamin peered through the holes of his enclosure at Emlee. Her leaf-green eyes looked at him with kindness.

Were these tulegs the same creatures that ordered the rumblers to tear through their ponds? The animals in Turtle Pond hated and feared the tulegs. Perhaps these "pets" were under a spell, prisoners of the evil tulegs. But if they were so evil, why did they coo at their pets, stroking their backs and holding them gently?

A tall tuleg with yellow fur and a white wrap appeared in one of the entranceways. It made a sound, and Emlee stood up, still clutching Benjamin's enclosure.

"Guh-guh-guh-good luck," said the guinea pig.

"Get better soon," purred the bobcat snuggled in its tuleg's lap.

"Hope you don't get a sharpie," yipped the small, white wolf in the corner.

"A sharpie?" asked Benjamin. The other animals winced and pursed their lips.

Before they could explain, Benjamin was whisked away into another room.

The yellow-furred tuleg spoke in its language to the tall Red tuleg who had come with Emlee. Then they all turned and looked at Benjamin. He fidgeted under their stare. Emlee opened the enclosure and lifted him out onto a cold, silver surface. It was hard and uncomfortable. Maybe this was the part that Cleo didn't like?

Next the yellow-furred tuleg reached over and poked at Benjamin. Benjamin pulled back, the pain from his injuries worsened by the prodding. The two taller tulegs spoke again, and Benjamin felt himself turned onto his back. Kicking his legs in the air, he began to understand why Cleo hated it at the vet. After more poking and prodding, the tuleg placed Benjamin back on his belly.

Benjamin's relief at being returned to the proper position quickly gave way to renewed fear as the yellow-furred tuleg grabbed a variety of sharp silver objects. Emlee pinned Benjamin to the table as the other tuleg scraped one of the objects against his shell. Wincing with pain from the pressure, Benjamin closed his eyes. The tuleg rubbed and rubbed, then rubbed some more. Benjamin wanted to shriek, but clenched his jaw instead.

Then the tuleg picked up a long, sharp object that resembled the quill of a porcupine. *A sharpie*, thought Benjamin. *Has to be.* The tuleg drove the sharpie through Benjamin's skin, causing a piercing pain. It was official: he hated going to the vet. The yellow-furred tuleg shoved yet another sharpie through Benjamin's tough skin. Immediately Benjamin felt a warm sensation invade his body. His head swam, and his vision blurred.

Soon the pain was gone. His fear was gone. The sharpie erased the deep ache in his body where the rumbler had hit him. Instead he felt happy, and daydreams of purple dragonflies, white lilies, and sweet red berries danced through his mind. Emlee stroked his head with her warm hands. Maybe the vet wasn't such a bad place after all.

Chapter 11

The Tea Party

"Was it terrible?" asked Cleo, floating against the wall of her tank.

Benjamin was drowsy and wanted to take a nap. But Cleo was so determined that he tried to answer. "Sometimes," he said, thinking about the scraping and the sharpies. "But not always," he added, remembering the moment when all of his pain disappeared.

"Do you want to play?" asked Cleo, bouncing against the tank wall with her nose.

"Not right now," said Benjamin. "I'm a little tired."

The last thing Benjamin saw before drifting off to sleep was Cleo's sad face, eager for a playmate. He slept the rest of the day and all night long. When he woke, his pain was back but wasn't as bad as before. Cleo was busy diving to the bottom of the deep side of her tank, pushing off, and springing to the surface over and over again. When she saw Benjamin awake, she darted over to the wall of her tank.

"You're awake!" she said.

"Yes, and I feel much better," said Benjamin.

"Maybe Emlee will take us outside to play," said Cleo.

"That would be great," said Benjamin, hoping for an opportunity to get back to Turtle Pond.

Emlee skipped through the door and sprinkled flakes of food into each of the tanks. Then she zipped around the room, gathering various objects. Her arms overflowing, she darted back out, leaving the turtles to scoop up the dry flakes in their mouths.

Emlee made several more trips in and out of the room while the turtles warmed themselves on their rocks. Then she stopped directly in front of their tanks. She reached in and lifted Benjamin out. He didn't struggle or resist, partially because he had grown to trust the small Red tuleg, but also because he knew he had a better chance of escaping from almost anywhere other than the tank.

Emlee placed Benjamin into a soft basket and reached up to get Cleo. For the first time since his arrival, he and Cleo were truly face to face—no more glass walls between them. They didn't have long together before Emlee gathered up the basket and left the room. She climbed down the stairs and ran across the tuleg den toward a large opening. As she stepped through the opening, Benjamin felt the sun on his back.

"We're outside!" he said.

Cleo smiled and nodded. "Emlee brings me out a lot. It's my favorite thing."

Benjamin took a full breath of air, enjoying the scent of the grass and flowers. While it didn't smell like Turtle Pond, it was much better than the heavy, unmoving odor of the tuleg den. A gentle breeze tickled his cheeks and chin. He lifted his nose into the air and smiled.

Emlee had arranged a number of her small, fake tulegs and fluffy, lifeless animals on small rocks around a large, round rock. A variety of objects and some bright red berries sat on the big rock.

"A party," said Cleo. "I love parties!"

"A party?" asked Benjamin. "With just you and me and Emlee?"

"Sshhhh," said Cleo. "Emlee thinks those other tulegs and animals are alive. They're at the party too! Besides, Horatio's usually here."

"Horatio?" asked Benjamin.

But before Cleo could answer, Emlee lifted her out of the basket and placed her on the large rock. Benjamin watched from inside the basket. Emlee grabbed some things from a sack near the rock and wrapped them around Cleo's shell. They looked like the soft wraps that tulegs wore around their bodies. Benjamin didn't know exactly what they were, but the closest things he could think of were lily pads, petals, and large maple leaves. When Emlee finished, she backed up to admire her work.

Benjamin had never seen Cleo look so proud. There she stood, her head held high, her shell wrapped in a fluffy white petal-thing with purple lines all over it. On her head sat a tiny basket decorated with a big, purple flower. *She looks ridiculous*, thought Benjamin, but he would never tell her so. She seemed so happy.

Emlee reached into the basket and pulled Benjamin onto the big rock. It was cold and smooth, unlike any rock he had felt before. Emlee slipped her fingers under him. He twisted his head to see what she was doing. She gathered a dainty pink petal, decorated with tiny rosebuds, around his body. Over his head she wrapped a blossom rimmed with fluffy white puffs. Benjamin looked at Cleo and the small fake tulegs. They looked like elaborate flowers with frilly little edges. Out of the corner of his eye, he caught sight of the white ruffle sitting on his own forehead. He hung his head, feeling about as silly as he had ever felt. He wondered what King Titus would think if he saw one of his strong young subjects dressed like a flower patch. He knew what Jeremiah would do. He would laugh so hard the pond would shake.

"You get used to it," said a voice from behind him.

Benjamin turned and found himself face to face with a large, leathery lizard. The lizard's wrap was as blue as the summer sky, with large white dots all over it. A lacey white petal covered his ear holes. His long, rugged tail protruded from beneath a piece of blue ruffle. While Cleo looked a little silly in her wrap, this tough, weatherworn lizard was the most ridiculous-looking thing he had ever seen. Stifling a laugh, Benjamin spoke.

"Who are you?" Benjamin asked.

"Horatio," said the lizard. He looked at Benjamin with one eye and the berries across the table with the other. "I'm an iguana, in case you're wondering."

"I was wondering, actually," admitted Benjamin.

"I'm from the South," said the iguana. "You're a red-eared slider, right? You're from the South too."

Benjamin had no idea where the South was, but he was pretty sure he wasn't from there. He was from Turtle Pond. "I don't think I'm from the South. I'm from Turtle Pond."

Horatio sighed. "Not you in particular. You as a species. Lots of sliders in the South."

Benjamin was interested. For as long as he could remember, he had been the only slider in Turtle Pond. Maybe he *was* from somewhere else. Maybe Gorn was right; maybe he wasn't like the others.

"Anyway, good to have you here," said Horatio, scratching at a loose piece of skin on his neck. "I usually have to wear the pink one. Charming on you, though."

Benjamin suddenly felt silly again. Here he was, possibly the prophesized new leader of Turtle Pond, dainty as a meadow flower.

Once he got past the humiliation of the pink, fluffy stuff wrapped around his body, Benjamin actually enjoyed himself. In the tank, he and Cleo only ate dry flakes. At the party, Emlee fed them fresh, plump berries that sprayed his tongue with sweet juice when he bit them. There were crunchy, orange vegetables, which were sweeter than he expected, and crisp, green leaves. Never before had Benjamin tasted such delicacies. He could see why Cleo liked the parties. The delicious treats were well worth the humiliation of the flowery petals wrapped around their bodies.

When he, Horatio, and Cleo had finished their feast, and Emlee was busy arranging her fake tulegs, Benjamin studied his surroundings. The rock on which they stood was far from the ground, but he could probably get down without damaging his shell. In any case, the fall couldn't possibly hurt as much as getting hit by a rumbler.

The rock sat in the middle of a large field, which was covered with the greenest grass Benjamin had ever seen. It was soft and smooth, with no rocks or bumps. He could move as quickly across that field as a turtle could move across anything. Beyond the grassy field, a patch of forest decorated the horizon. Whether the forest was big or small, near his pond or far from it, Benjamin couldn't tell. But if he reached the woods, he could hide in the bushes so that Emlee couldn't put him back in his tank. From there he would figure out where to go. He would walk and walk until he saw something, anything, familiar. Even if he had to walk for a month, he would find his way back to Turtle Pond.

If it was still there.

Benjamin turned to Cleo. Her chin dripped with sweet, red juice.

"Cleo, I have to leave. It's been great to meet you, but I have to find my way back to Turtle Pond."

Cleo pouted. "But you just got here. Can't you stay a little longer?"

"No. Turtle Pond is in danger from the rumblers. I don't know whether I can help my friends in the pond or not, but I've got to try."

Cleo's eyes moistened. "But you're my only friend." She turned and looked at Emlee, who was pulling something green and silky around the neck of a fake bobcat. Horatio watched her, the dewlap under his chin moving in and out. Cleo smiled. "Well, my only turtle friend, anyway."

Benjamin liked Cleo. It was nice to meet another red-eared slider after being the only slider in Turtle Pond for so long. Suddenly he had an idea. "Come with me," he said. "Come back with me to Turtle Pond."

Cleo's eyes brightened, but only for a moment. She looked at Emlee and at the sweet bits of leftover berries on the rock. "I'd love to…really I would. But I can't leave Emlee. And besides, I'm scared. This is my home. I don't want to leave."

"I understand," said Benjamin, remembering how the animals at the vet had cuddled with their tulegs.

He walked over to the edge of the rock and looked down. Horatio saw him there and came over.

"Gonna make a break for it?" the iguana asked, picking at some loose skin on his tail.

"Yes," said Benjamin. "I've got to get back to my pond."

"I made a break for it once," said Horatio. "Made it as far as those trees. But at night, it was awfully cold. There were wild creatures with long teeth and black rings round their eyes. Worst, there were no berries. I came back the next day."

Horatio rolled one eye up to look at his white, lacy head wrap. "It's worth it," he said.

Benjamin pushed his jaw against the white petal tied under his chin. It wouldn't budge. He grinned at the large lizard. "Well, at least I'll be taking the pink wrap with me."

"And for that, I'm eternally grateful," said Horatio. "Happy trails, young slider."

Benjamin turned. Emlee was still busy on the other side of the rock. It was now or never. He pushed with his back legs, then pulled his legs and head into his shell to protect them from damage. Tumbling down, he braced for the worst. Fortunately the bright green grass was not only beautiful, but soft. Uninjured, Benjamin whipped out his legs and scrambled toward the trees. *I'm a wolf dashing through the meadow*, he thought. *A rumbler. I can run like the eagle flies.*

But he couldn't. Try as he might, Benjamin only made it halfway across the soft field before he felt the rhythmic vibration of Emlee's feet against the ground. Apparently tulegs were faster than turtles too.

Chapter 12

Paradise

The following day, Emlee jumped out of her nest before the dawn's soft, pink rays snuck into the room. Benjamin followed her with his eyes as she pulled on her wraps, spun around in full circles four times, and darted out the door.

"Cleo," Benjamin whispered. When he was met with silence, he tried again, raising his voice. "*Cleo!*"

Horatio's gruff voice cut the early morning air. "Some of us are trying to sleep."

"Leave him alone, Horatio," said Cleo, emerging from behind her rock. "What's going on, Benjamin?"

Benjamin paddled over to the clear wall of his tank. "Emlee's up early. She seems excited."

"I hope we're going outside," Cleo said.

Benjamin was hoping too. He had to try again to reach Turtle Pond.

Emlee returned and busied herself with the basket she had used to take them outside the day before. Benjamin's heart flooded with hope. He was going to get a second chance to get back to the pond that very day.

It wasn't long before Benjamin, Cleo, and Horatio wobbled in their basket as Emlee sprinted down the stairs of the tuleg den. This time the two big tulegs stood in front of their home, waiting for Emlee to appear. The tall Red tuleg wore a green covering with a big maple leaf on it and carried a large sack.

Maybe they were going somewhere different today.

Emlee climbed into the rumbler, bringing the basket with her. Benjamin looked around the now-familiar belly of the rumbler and felt happy that Cleo and Horatio were there with him.

"Where do you think we're going?" asked Benjamin.

"I don't know," said Cleo. "Emlee doesn't bring me into the rumbler very often."

"Doesn't much matter to me," said Horatio. "So long as there are berries."

Emlee pushed down on a pebble next to her, and a crack appeared in the shell of the rumbler. Through the crack, a strong, cool breeze whirled into the compartment. Benjamin and Cleo pushed their heads into the wind, enjoying the fresh air racing against their faces. At first the air was crisp, but unfamiliar. Before long the strong scent of pine trees blew in. Then the gentle odors of maple and oak and hickory reached Benjamin's nose. Hints of sweet wildflower wove in and out of his nostrils. He smiled at Cleo, and she smiled back.

Suddenly Benjamin's smile dissolved, leaving an urgent look on his face. He smelled something familiar…the unmistakable scent of pond.

"What is it?" asked Cleo.

"Probably constipated," offered Horatio. "I always get that look on my face when I can't go to the bathroom."

"The pond," said Benjamin. "I smell the pond."

He craned his neck, peering through the clear parts of the rumbler's shell. His jaw dropped. Up ahead, approaching rapidly, was the Big Oak. Ever since Benjamin had been a very young turtle in the pond, sunning himself on the mossy log, he had viewed the Big Oak as a symbol of strength. Rising to the sky at the north end of Turtle Pond, it was always there, always straight, always keeping watch over the pond.

"Where?" asked Cleo.

Benjamin's heart beat quickly. "Here. I mean, out there. The rumbler is running past Turtle Pond. We're on Rumbler Run."

But as quickly as the Big Oak appeared, it disappeared. The rumbler slowed and turned away from the spot where the pond should have been. It made its way deeper into the forest. Through the clear rumbler shell, Benjamin and Cleo saw more and more trees. Horatio, on the other hand, was busy tugging on a loose piece of skin dangling from his tail and didn't really care where they were.

The rumbler stopped, and the tall Red tuleg opened the shell, freeing Emlee, Benjamin, Cleo, and Horatio from its belly.

"We're in the forest!" said Cleo, her eyes wide with wonder. "We don't come here very often."

Benjamin's mind was already busy with a plan. They had gone a long way from Emlee's den before they passed Turtle Pond. But they had turned into this forest almost immediately after that. They were close…very close. Suddenly Benjamin was glad he hadn't escaped during the party. It could have taken him weeks, or even months, to get home from Emlee's den. Would the pond have still been there? But from here, it would take only days…maybe.

The tulegs spread a large, soft object, almost like a lily pad, over the ground. It was made with long threads of orange, red, and burgundy and felt good against Benjamin's feet when Emlee lifted him down. Soon Cleo and Horatio stood on the sunset-colored pad with him.

"Where are the berries?" asked Horatio.

"A picnic!" said Cleo. "We're having a picnic!"

"What's a picnic?" asked Benjamin.

"It's like a tea party, but with no flowery wraps and hats," said Cleo.

"It's perfection," said Horatio.

Sure enough the sunset pad was soon covered with all sorts of tuleg foods, including—to Horatio's delight—berries. The turtles and iguana sat with the tulegs, enjoying their meal. The berries had never tasted so sweet, and Benjamin liked the way Emlee nestled close to him. Her long, warm legs were almost like a hot, mossy log on a summer day. Near the end of the meal, one of the big tulegs opened a large basket and pulled out some packets.

"Shiners!" gasped Benjamin.

"Pardon me?" asked Horatio.

"Shiners," said Benjamin. "Those things the tulegs just pulled out are shiners."

Horatio and Cleo looked at each other and shrugged. The tulegs tore open the shiners and put them onto the sunset pad. They were lovely shiners: sleek silver on one side, colorful symbols on the other. When the sun caught them just right, they reflected back the light with such brilliance that Benjamin had to squint. While the tulegs ate whatever had been inside the shiners, Benjamin snuck over and grabbed one in his mouth. He tucked it under his shell where no one could see it. It would make a fine gift for Wibble, if he ever saw him again.

After the meal, Emlee put the turtles and iguana back into their basket and followed the tall Red tuleg wearing the green maple leaf through the woods. They soon reached a clearing, and Emlee lifted Benjamin, Cleo, and Horatio onto a sunny spot in the grass.

Benjamin's nostrils flared. "A pond!" He turned around. There it was: the most beautiful pond he had ever seen. It was five times bigger than Turtle Pond, with dozens of soft logs jutting from the clear water into the sun. Lily pads lined one side, their silky, white flowers trembling in the morning breeze. Blue and purple dragonflies chased one another through the tall weeds, and water bugs skated across the surface on their long legs.

"Paradise," murmured Benjamin.

Cleo and Horatio turned to look. "It's beautiful!" said Cleo.

"It's home," said Benjamin.

Chapter 13

The Last Great Escape Plan

Horatio closed one eye and looked at the pond with the other. "Doesn't look like paradise to me."

"You're an iguana; I'm a turtle. To me it's paradise. In any case, to a pond about to be destroyed by rumblers, it's a miracle."

Near the shore, a small, spotted turtle climbed onto a sunny log.

"What's that thing?" asked Horatio.

"It's a spotted turtle," Benjamin said. A week earlier, he wouldn't have known either.

"Come on," Benjamin said. "I need to ask him something."

Cleo followed Benjamin to the edge of the pond while Horatio stayed in the clearing to scratch his itchy skin.

"Hello there," Benjamin said. "My name is Benjamin, and this is my friend Cleo."

"Pleased to meet you," said the spotted turtle. "My name is Spotz."

"Are there many turtles in this pond?" asked Benjamin.

"It's a lake," said Spotz, "and there are very few turtles, because it's a new lake. It was made by the beaver family just two seasons ago."

Benjamin peered across the lake at the fresh beaver dam.

"Do you think it would be OK if I came back with some other turtles? Our pond is being destroyed, and we need a new home."

Spotz smiled from ear to ear. "It's not just OK—it's great! There's so much room here, and only a few turtles. It would be wonderful to have some new friends."

Spotz suddenly fell silent. He darted from the log into the water. "Good-bye," he yelled from a safe distance.

Benjamin turned around and found himself face to face with Horatio.

"Skittish little thing, isn't he?" said Horatio.

"Guess he's never seen an iguana before," said Benjamin. "I didn't realize you were so scary."

"It's a talent," said Horatio.

Benjamin's face grew serious. "I have to get my friends from Turtle Pond and bring them to this lake. You heard Spotz—there's plenty of room for more turtles. I think I can make it home from here."

Cleo's eyes dimmed. "Do you have to go today?"

Benjamin sighed. "The pond could already be gone, Cleo…or if it's still there, the rumblers could destroy it today, or tomorrow. I can't take any chances. I have to go now. I need a plan."

Benjamin looked at Emlee and the other Red tuleg. They were crouched by the water, scooping up drops in long containers. Emlee turned to check on her animal friends every few minutes, but her back was to them most of the time. All along the edge of the lake were grassy tufts and, just beyond those, untouched forest. There were no tulegs, no Rumbler Runs, and no tuleg dens anywhere in sight. If Benjamin could make it to the forest, he could get away into the wild. About ten steps away, a cluster of tall weeds sprung from the ground. Benjamin had an idea.

He turned to Horatio and Cleo. "We've got to stack."

Horatio yawned. "Pardon me?"

"We've got to stack," repeated Benjamin. "Sometimes, when the sunny log gets crowded, the younger turtles crawl on top of each other in a pile."

Cleo wrinkled her snout. "A stack sounds like fun, but how will that help you get away?"

"Because I'll get at the bottom of the stack in that pile of weeds over there. Emlee won't be able to see me, but if she knows I'm there, she won't look for me."

Cleo's eyes widened. "And then you'll just slip off the bottom."

Benjamin smiled. "Right."

Horatio stretched one of his front legs. "Well, I'm willing, so long as I can take a nap."

"Can you take a nap on my back?" Benjamin asked.

Horatio studied Benjamin's shell. "Not sure about that. Seems sort of curvy."

Benjamin begged Horatio with his eyes. "Please, Horatio."

Horatio rolled one eye. "Very well. I'll try my best."

Benjamin crept over to the grassy tuft and waited until Emlee turned and saw him standing there. Then he signaled for Horatio to climb onto him.

Horatio groaned. "I can't say I recommend turtle-sleeping. It's like having a rock stuck in your stomach. You should wait at least an hour after eating to crawl up on a turtle."

"Shhh, Horatio," whispered Cleo, grabbing onto his flaky tail with her front claws.

Horatio shut his eyes and raised his chin. "But your claws feel good against my shedding skin."

Cleo smiled and scratched her claws all over Horatio's back on her way up. They stood in their turtle-iguana-turtle pile long enough for Emlee to turn and notice them. She pointed at them, and the larger Red tuleg turned to look. It showed its teeth, and so did Emlee. Benjamin wasn't afraid. He knew what that meant. Tulegs showed their teeth when they were happy, not when they were hungry.

"OK," said Benjamin. "It's time."

Benjamin twisted and turned his body, trying to slip out from underneath Horatio. The lizard's large body teetered on Benjamin's shifting shell.

"Worse than an earthquake," said Horatio. "I don't think I like stacking."

Cleo dug her claws into Horatio's back to keep from falling.

Horatio winced. "I definitely don't like stacking."

At last Benjamin slipped out from under Horatio, sending the old iguana crashing to the ground.

"That hurt," said Horatio.

"Sorry," said Benjamin. "I tried to be gentle."

"I know, I know," said Horatio. "Curvy shell and all that. Couldn't be helped."

Cleo looked at Benjamin with sad eyes. "So I guess this is good-bye, huh?"

Benjamin smiled at her. "Yes, but I'll never forget you, Cleo. You've been a good friend."

"Best make a break for it while the going's good," said Horatio.

Benjamin took one last look at the leathery, old lizard and the small girl turtle teetering on his peeling back. Then he turned into the weeds and scurried away. Behind him he heard Cleo sniffle. Horatio urged him onward. "Run like the wind! Never look back!"

Benjamin ran. He looked straight ahead and moved his legs in a steady rhythm. *I've got to make it*, he thought. *The other turtles need me.* But run as he might, it was only minutes before he felt the familiar *thud, thud, thud* of Emlee's feet pounding the ground behind him. Her warm fingers wrapped around his shell, unraveling his hope. *I'll never get back*, he thought. His heart flooded with despair.

The tall Red tuleg walked over and stood next to Emlee. It shook its head and made strange noises. Emlee answered the tall tuleg, her tone desperate. Benjamin wondered what they were saying. Emlee's teeth didn't show. Droplets of water fell from her eyes.

Emlee turned and walked over to the lake, holding Benjamin close to her warm body. The tall tuleg wrapped an arm around her, and they both lowered themselves to the ground next to the water. *What are they going to do to me?* Benjamin thought. *They must be angry that I tried to escape.*

Salty tears rolled off Emlee's face and splashed Benjamin's nose. She placed him, belly down, into the shallow water at the edge of the lake. The tall tuleg nodded and pulled Emlee close. She opened her fingers, releasing Benjamin from her grip. He was free.

Benjamin darted a few feet into the lake and ducked under a bit of log. He peeked out at the tulegs. Emlee stared at him, her Hopper-green eyes brimming with sorrow. Benjamin felt sorry for her. She didn't want to let him go. The big tuleg had made her do it. He studied the face of the tall Red tuleg. It understood. Somehow it knew that Benjamin needed to be free, and it made Emlee release him.

Maybe tulegs weren't so bad after all. No, they definitely weren't so bad after all.

Benjamin's tulegs stood and turned away from the lake. Emlee bent down and scooped up Cleo and Horatio on the way back to the picnic spot. Benjamin watched her red fur swing back and forth as she walked.

"Good-bye, little Red tuleg," he whispered. "Good-bye, Emlee."

Chapter 14

Rustles in the Night

Benjamin looked at the sky. There was still time left before the sun disappeared. He had to get going. Turtle Pond could already be gone.

In his head, he retraced the path Emlee's rumbler had taken. If he followed the setting sun toward the west, he would reach Rumbler Run. Then he would have to face the Run once more to get home to the pond.

Benjamin moved quickly to cover as much territory as he could before the daylight disappeared. He planned to travel through the

night, but would have to be careful when it got dark. It would be
hard to see where he was going, and there would be dangerous predators. The *scratch, rustle, scratch* of his feet moving through the dry
leaves on the forest floor set the cadence for his journey. He walked
and walked and walked, always thinking about his friends in Turtle
Pond. Had Hopper found Wibble? Were Kip and Dot recovering?
Was the pond still there? Soon his nagging thoughts were replaced by
a nagging ache over one front leg. Why did that leg hurt so much
more than the others?

Benjamin stopped and wiggled his sore shoulder. The glossy, silver
shiner tumbled to the ground. He had almost forgotten about the
beautiful shiner he had saved for Wibble. For a moment, he wondered if he should abandon it in the woods. Would it slow him down?
But then he tucked it neatly under his shell on the opposite side. It
would give Wibble such pleasure. He had to keep it. Just in case.

Benjamin forged onward. Soon pink ribbons crawled across the
darkening sky, and the chirping of crickets filled the air. Night was
coming. He would need to be more careful—no more *scratch-scratch-
ing* through the leaves. The sound would attract predators. He would
have to stretch one leg forward at a time, lifting his belly above the
ground so that he could glide silently ahead. It would be slow going.

Darkness fell, and still Benjamin traveled. During an especially
long reach of one front leg, he thought he heard a sound in the
bushes beside him. He froze. Was it his imagination? He listened
carefully. No, it wasn't. There was definitely something there. It too
crept slowly. Was it stalking him?

Benjamin didn't dare move. His front leg ached from its awkward
posture, but he couldn't pull it back; the thing in the bushes might
hear him. He held his breath. The rustle in the bushes stopped. Did
it see him? Was it preparing to pounce? He wondered what it was.
Could it be a giant owl, its sharp claws drawn, preparing to tear

through his flesh? Perhaps a wolf with sharp, gleaming teeth? His legs trembled. How much longer could he remain frozen in this position?

The bushes sprang to life. Its branches parted, and Benjamin saw something rush toward him. His heart pounded hard against his chest. Should he run? He could never outrun an owl or a wolf. Maybe it hadn't seen him. The shadow was almost on him, but with no moon in the sky, he couldn't see what it was. Panicked, he did the only thing he could think of: he pulled his head and legs into his shell.

Something jarred him, and then a small *patter-pat* pounded his back like hard rain.

"Benjamin! Benjamin, is that you?"

He shot his head out of his shell. He knew that voice.

"Hopper! Hopper, is that you?"

A second voice cried out. "Benjamin! You're alive!"

"Wibble?" Benjamin's fear dissolved into joy. There was no predator in the bushes; it was Hopper and Wibble.

The three friends huddled together near the bush, overwhelmed by their unexpected reunion.

"How did you get over here?" asked Benjamin.

Hopper bounced around in the leaves. "It was Wibble, really. I found him the night after he disappeared. He was hiding alone in the woods under a raspberry bush."

"Snacks and shelter at once," said Wibble.

"Anyway, it took us until the next day to get back, because you turtles aren't exactly the fastest animals in the forest."

Wibble huffed.

Hopper persisted. "We got back the afternoon after you tried to cross the Run. The other turtles told Wibble that you disappeared. They didn't know where you were. Some said a tuleg took you. Others said you crawled away from the tuleg to the other side of the Run. A few swore that the tuleg put you down across the Run."

Benjamin was eager to tell his story, but he let Hopper finish.

"So Wibble said he was going to try to cross the Run to find you, but King Titus wouldn't let him. He said enough turtles had been destroyed by the Run and declared it impossible to cross. He formed three committees to look into the problem of getting the turtles to safety."

Benjamin rolled his eyes. "They're probably still meeting."

"Probably," agreed Wibble.

Hopper jumped up and down faster as the climax of the story approached.

"Shhh," said Wibble. "You'll attract an owl."

Hopper tried to calm down but was exploding with a good tale. "Anyway, Wibble told me he was going to try the Run anyway. So he waited until deep into the night, after all the other turtles were asleep."

This time it was Wibble who couldn't contain himself: "And then I crossed the Run. Just like that. Just walked right across. Not a single rumbler. Me. I crossed the Run."

Hopper fidgeted. "And me. I hopped across with him." He turned to Benjamin. "I promised you that I would get Wibble back for you, and I wasn't about to let him get squashed by a rumbler."

Benjamin smiled. "Wow. I can't believe it. You're both so brave. You could've been killed."

Hopper bobbed up and down on his hind legs. "Could've been killed? It was almost a certainty! The most dangerous thing anyone could've done. But we did it. That's right...me and Wibble. By ourselves. Not a moment of fear."

Benjamin knew Wibble well enough to suspect otherwise, and Wibble had no desire to pretend.

"Scared to death, actually," admitted Wibble. "My legs shook all the way across. But they said you might be on the other side. My best friend. How could I just leave you over here by yourself? I had to come and find you. So I did."

Warmth flowed through Benjamin's cold body. Wibble had risked his life just to find him. He felt lucky to have friends like Hopper and Wibble, no matter what Gorn said.

"You guys are the best friends a turtle could have," said Benjamin.

A sudden gust of wind, ominous in its silence, flew over their heads. The loud squeal of a field mouse reached their ears.

"Owl," whispered Wibble. "We'd better get under cover."

The strange trio of friends crawled under the bush.

"Let's keep going," said Benjamin. "We need to get back quickly."

"It's slow going at night," said Wibble. "There are predators."

"We can't waste any time," said Benjamin. "It could take us a while to find our way back."

Hopper's voice practically exploded. "Tell him, Wibble. Tell him."

Wibble leaned close to Benjamin so the owl wouldn't hear. "We left a trail. A trail of shiners. It leads us straight home."

Chapter 15

Along the Shiner Trail

Benjamin smiled. Wibble had never before shown as much courage as he had the past few days, but intelligence was another thing entirely. Wibble had always been a clever turtle, so his shiner plan came as no surprise.

Wibble continued the story of his adventure with Hopper.

"We moved slowly, searching the underbrush carefully for any signs of you, or"—Wibble swallowed hard—"your shell."

"But we've only been gone for about a day and a half," said Hopper, "and we hid at night instead of traveling."

Benjamin's hopes soared. They were close to home. "So we could make it back to the pond by tomorrow night if we hurry."

"I think so," said Wibble.

The turtles and frog did travel that night, but they moved slowly and rested often, taking naps under the bushes. Because Benjamin was the only turtle who knew the way to the new lake, Wibble and Hopper insisted on taking no chances. The turtles of Turtle Pond were doomed if the trio of friends died in the jaws of a wolf pack.

It felt like a long time before the eastern sky finally grew pale from the glow of approaching sunlight. Benjamin was surprised at how good it felt to once again lay eyes on Hopper's shimmery green skin and Wibble's muddy shell. Wibble must have used up most of his shiners making the trail, because only two or three remained attached to his back. The sad state of his friend's shiner collection reminded Benjamin about the gift he bore under his shell.

"Wibble?"

Wibble turned and smiled. "Yes, Benjamin?"

"I've got something for you." Benjamin wiggled his shoulder, and the brilliant shiner fell to the ground. It landed with the duller side, containing colorful tuleg symbols, face up. Wibble's eyes grew wide.

"It's magnificent!" he exclaimed. "It's the most beautiful shiner I've ever seen!"

"Turn it over," suggested Benjamin.

Hopper used his powerful back legs to flip the shiner over for Wibble. The sun struck its surface, and a blinding light reflected back. The turtles scrunched their eyes closed.

"That's got to be the brightest shiner in the world," said Wibble, smiling under his squint. He scooped it up in his mouth and tucked it carefully under his own shell. "Thank you, Benjamin."

Benjamin smiled. No other turtle in the world would care about such a thing. But Wibble wasn't like any other turtle in the world.

As they embarked on their journey along Wibble's shiner trail, Benjamin told his friends all about Cleo, Horatio, and Emlee. He explained about pets, nice tulegs, and riding in rumblers. Hopper's eyes were alive with interest, and Wibble's mouth hung open wide, closing only when he needed to rearrange one of his precious shiners along the path.

By the time the sun was high in the sky, Benjamin had finished his story. The three friends walked silently; they were hungry, thirsty, and tired. But instead of looking for a berry bush or a nice puddle of water, they kept moving. Their legs grew weary, and even Hopper's jumping lost altitude. Other than the shuffle of their feet against the ground, the only sounds were occasional grunts or groans as someone's foot hit a sharp twig. As the sun dropped toward the western horizon, Benjamin wondered how much longer they could keep up such an unrelenting pace. Hopper's skin was puckering, and they would need to find him water.

Benjamin stopped. "We've got to find water."

Wibble turned, a smile spreading across his face. "We nearly have."

Hopper leaped into the air, landing on Benjamin's shell. "We're here!"

Benjamin looked up. In front of them was a large hill. At the top of the hill, strong gusts of wind forced pebbles over the edge every few seconds. Under his feet, the ground grumbled in concert with the flying gravel. They had reached Rumbler Run.

"How did we get here so quickly?" he asked.

"We weren't that far," said Wibble. "Once the sun came up, we never stopped. We never took a break."

Benjamin looked at Hopper's parched skin. They had followed the sun westward all day—never slowing, never resting, never faltering.

Their legs were sore, and their mouths were dry, but it had been worth it. Turtle Pond, if it was still there, was just on the other side of Rumbler Run.

Wibble stared straight ahead. Benjamin knew what that meant: that meant he was thinking. Finally Wibble spoke.

"Hopper and I got across Rumbler Run very late at night. It was probably not far from dawn. There were fewer rumblers then. We need to wait."

They were so close to Turtle Pond that Benjamin could smell it. The familiar scent of the algae and moss rotting at the surface of the pond reached his nose. A delicate mixture of lilies and maple danced on the breeze. Benjamin desperately wanted to be home to see that everything was OK. But he knew the pond was still there. It lacked the strong, rich scent of soil freshly unearthed by rumblers. Its aroma was full of life…just as it should be.

"All right," said Benjamin. "You're right. We've got to wait. But we really need to find water." He lowered his voice, "I'm worried about Hopper."

"I heard that," croaked Hopper through his dry mouth. "I'm just fine. I can jump through the woods for days without water. Don't worry about me." With each word, Hopper's voice cracked more.

"I see what you mean," whispered Wibble. He raised his voice. "Well, I can see that Hopper's fine, but I'm going to die of thirst if I don't get some water. I'll never make it across Rumbler Run."

Hopper lay sprawled on his belly against the cool soil of the forest floor. "Well, if *you* need water, we must find some." His voice trailed off.

Benjamin walked over to the limp frog. "The back of my shell is terribly hot from the sunny day we had today, Hopper. Be a pal and lay your cool body on my shell, would you?"

Hopper cleared his throat. "Anything for a friend." With the last bit of his energy, he leaped onto Benjamin's back.

"Thanks, Hopper," said Benjamin.

Wibble left an extra shiner next to the spot across from Turtle Pond, but Benjamin knew it wasn't necessary. The tall oak stood guard in the distance, and the sweet smells of the pond blew across the Run. No shiner could mark the right place better than that.

Benjamin and Wibble walked along the base of the hill, looking for water. By the time they found a small spring, they had already traveled several hours. The sky was dark, lit only by the light of the crescent moon. The air was crisp, and crickets chirped in steady rhythm. Hopper was still and silent.

"Hopper?" Benjamin asked.

Wibble moved over to look at the small frog. "He's not moving."

"*Hopper?*" Benjamin yelled.

"Shhh," said Wibble. "The owls."

"Is he alive?" asked Benjamin, his voice shrill.

"I can't tell," said Wibble. "Let's dump him into the puddle and see what happens."

Benjamin figured this plan was as good as any other, so he bent down near the small, deep pool and tipped his body. Hopper slid off his back and landed with a dull splash in the water. Benjamin and Wibble huddled together at the edge of the pool and stared into its depths. There was no movement. A lump rose in Benjamin's throat. Hopper had to be OK. He just had to be.

"Is he…" Wibble asked.

"Shhh," said Benjamin. "He's fine. I'm sure of it." But Benjamin wasn't sure of it. Hopper's body had slid off his back with no resistance…dead weight.

Benjamin gazed so far into the still, dark water that his nose touched the surface. A sudden explosion from the depths sent him reeling back so hard that he bent his tail against the ground.

"Just what I needed!" yelled Hopper, bouncing back and forth from Benjamin's shell to Wibble's.

The turtles laughed, their fear pounded away by the small wet feet of their frog friend. They all dove into the water and swam to the bottom, where they drank and played until the sliver of moon was high in the sky.

They pulled their dripping bodies out of the small pool. "It's time to head back to the crossing spot," said Benjamin.

"I guess it is," said Wibble, his voice shaking. Wibble was not the sort of turtle to assume that one successful trip across Rumbler Run meant that a second crossing would be safe.

"It'll be OK," said Benjamin, thinking how much courage it must have taken for his normally fearful friend to cross the Run. "Really."

But crossing the Run was not to be among their adventures that night, for at that moment, Benjamin heard a sound.

Chapter 16

The Voice in the Air

"What was that?" asked Benjamin.

"What was what?" replied Wibble.

The three friends stood frozen in place, each stretching their necks to try to hear the sound.

A faint, high-pitched echo traveled to them on the cool evening breeze.

"Did you hear that?" asked Benjamin.

"Yes," said Wibble. "I did hear it that time. What do you suppose it is?"

Benjamin raised his head into the wind. He heard it again. It was a distant sound, one that he might ignore were it not, somehow, familiar.

"Let's ignore it and get going," said Hopper. "It's probably a mouse running from a bobcat."

"No," said Benjamin. "It's not. It's…it's…" A part of his brain knew what it was, but that part of his brain wasn't talking to his mouth. What was it? No…*who* was it?

Benjamin stammered again. "It's…it's…Dot!" He hadn't known the answer until that very moment.

"Are you sure?" asked Wibble.

"Why would she be out in the woods in the middle of the night?" asked Hopper.

"I don't know," said Benjamin. "But I intend to find out."

"But what about Rumbler Run?" asked Hopper. Now that he had his strength back, he was ready for action.

"Dot first," said Benjamin. He was the one Dot had landed on when the rumblers tossed her across the Great Divide, and that made him responsible for her.

Wibble nodded. "OK. I guess we still have some time. Besides, I wasn't really looking forward to standing around waiting to cross."

The part of the Run near Turtle Pond was somewhere behind them, but Dot's distant yell was coming from ahead of them. Benjamin, renewed from their swim, took off in the direction of her voice. Wibble and Hopper followed.

As they moved, the distant yelling became more sporadic, but louder. Each time they heard Dot's voice, Benjamin quickened his pace. Soon Wibble was having trouble keeping up.

"Are you sure we should keep heading away from the pond?" he asked, gasping for breath.

"No," said Benjamin, "I'm not sure, but we've got to find Dot. What if she's in trouble?"

"What if the pond's in trouble?" asked Hopper.

Benjamin stopped. Then he started again. "Dot wouldn't leave the pond if it were in trouble. Not unless she took everyone with her."

Wibble could see there was no arguing with Benjamin, so he followed, doing his best to keep up with the rapid walking. Hopper jumped along at a strong pace, more convinced with each hop that there was sure to be adventure ahead.

"We'll save her," Hopper said. "I'm not afraid. No matter what's going on, we'll save her."

Benjamin smiled at the serious face of his green friend. "We sure will," he said.

The moon was sinking in the sky before they drew close enough to the voice to make out what it was saying. "Benjamin! Wibble! Hopper!"

Benjamin froze and turned to his friends. Wibble caught up, huffing and puffing.

"She's calling us," said Benjamin. "She's out in the middle of the night looking for us! What if a wolf gets her?"

Totally disregarding the possibility that a wolf could get him too, Benjamin cried out in his loudest voice. "Dot! Dot, it's Benjamin!"

There was silence ahead. Benjamin tried again. "Dot! Dot!"

The distant yelling became louder and more urgent. "Benjamin! Benjamin!"

Benjamin took off in the direction of the yelling, revitalized by their interaction. Even Wibble felt stronger, energized by the sense that they had all found one another. Hopper leaped into the air and darted ahead, following Dot's cry. With each degree that the moon sank in the sky, her voice drew closer. At last Benjamin and Wibble had the sense that they were almost on top of Dot, but she was nowhere in sight.

"Where are you, Dot?" Benjamin called.

"Nearby somewhere. Where are you?" she replied.

"We're near a big tree," yelled Benjamin.

"There aren't any big trees near us," she hollered back.

"Us?" asked Wibble.

"Are you alone?" asked Benjamin.

"No," yelled Dot. "Are you near a raspberry bush?"

It was dark, and there were shadows all around. Wibble spun in circles, searching for anything shaped like a raspberry bush. He shook his head at Benjamin.

"I don't think so," answered Benjamin. She sounded so close. He couldn't understand why they weren't seeing any of the same things. Just then Hopper landed on his back.

"Ask her if she's near a tunnel," he said.

Benjamin looked at Hopper, confused.

"Just ask her," he said.

"Are you near a tunnel?" asked Benjamin.

Silence filled the night. Where had she gone? Was she looking for the tunnel? Benjamin started to worry. The hooting of an owl echoed across the sky. Was she under attack? Maybe she was just staying quiet until it passed.

Suddenly the sound of her voice rang through the air again. "Yes! Yes we are!"

Hopper leaped in front of Benjamin and grinned in the dim light of the moon. "Follow me," he whispered.

Benjamin and Wibble hurried along behind Hopper. He stopped about thirty steps ahead. At the base of the hill, running under Rumbler Run, was a small, dark tunnel.

"Are you still there?" yelled Dot.

Her voice was so loud that Benjamin and Wibble jumped back. But Dot wasn't anywhere near the tunnel. Her voice came from the other side. Benjamin stuck his head into the tunnel. He lowered his voice.

"Yes, we're here," he said.

"Where are you?"

"I think we're on the other side of the tunnel."

"Across Rumbler Run?" Dot asked.

That explained it. Dot hadn't crossed Rumbler Run. She was on the pond side.

"Yes," replied Benjamin. He turned and looked at Wibble and Hopper. His friends had been through so much already. They had crossed Rumbler Run. They had spent almost two days searching the woods for him. Then they had marched through the forest so relentlessly that Hopper had nearly died. How could he ask them to do it?

"I'm going under," he said.

Hopper raised his chin and leaped to his side. "Then I'm going too."

Benjamin expected nothing less from Hopper. He turned to Wibble. "You don't have to come with us. It could be dangerous."

"It will be dangerous," said Hopper. "Guaranteed."

Wibble walked over and stood between his friends. His voice trembled, but he held his head high. "You think I'm going to let you have all the fun?"

"Stay there," Benjamin said to Dot. "We're coming to you."

"Be careful!" she said.

The turtles and frog turned and faced the unknown dangers of the tunnel.

Chapter 17

Through the Long Darkness

"I've never seen such darkness," said Wibble, his voice shaking.

"Just move slowly," said Benjamin.

The bottom of the tunnel was covered with a thin layer of water that splashed under their feet. The passage was narrow, but big enough for young turtles to walk through without scraping their shells on the side. It stank of stagnant water and rusty metal.

Occasionally a sharp bit of loose metal tore against the foot of one of the turtles, enhancing the sense of danger.

"Get up on my back," Benjamin said to Hopper.

"Why? I'm not afraid," said Hopper.

"I know that," said Benjamin. "But there's something sharp on the bottom, and your skin is thinner than mine. No point in both of us getting hurt."

"Can I get on your back too?" teased Wibble, cringing from a particularly sharp bit of metal. "Really, Hopper, you're not doing anyone any favors. What if we need someone to get help really fast when we get to the other side?"

Hopper sighed and jumped onto Benjamin's back. It was hard for him to sit still, so he busied himself shifting to and fro, looking for any sign of light.

"I feel like there's a sac of frog eggs hatching on my back," said Benjamin. "Can you settle down up there?" He laughed, trying to keep the mood cheerful. But no amount of joking could lighten the atmosphere. Every sound they made was distorted into spooky echoes by the metal walls. The *scratch*, *splash* of their feet against the bottom whirled into a low snarl. And every few minutes, the whole tunnel tossed and vibrated as a rumbler thundered by overhead.

Dot's high-pitched voice echoed through the darkness. "Are you in there?"

"Yes," said Benjamin. "But I'm not sure how far we are."

"Be careful," said Dot.

Benjamin narrowed his eyes, searching for any sign of light. Nothing. It was dark as midnight.

A sudden squeal broke his concentration. Hopper leaped off Benjamin's back and landed neatly on Wibble's, following the sound of the scream.

Benjamin stopped and spoke to Wibble through the darkness. "Did you cut your foot?"

Wibble's words shook. "There's something in here with us."

Hopper answered, his voice crisp and courageous. "Well, it won't get us, that's for sure. Where is it? I'll protect you, Wibble."

Benjamin wished he could see Hopper's small, green body on Wibble's broad back. He imagined one froggy foot curled into a fist.

"What did you hear?" asked Benjamin.

"I didn't hear anything. I felt it."

That's worse, thought Benjamin. *That means it's close to us.*

Wibble shrieked again and ran forward, crashing into the back of Benjamin's shell. Hopper flew off and landed in the water with a loud splash. A suffocating sense of panic filled the tunnel.

Benjamin's voice faltered. "Wibble, please try to stay calm."

"I can't," said Wibble. "It's right here. It just…eeeeee!"

Benjamin felt it too: something long and smooth slithered by, rubbing against his legs. It hugged one of his feet with an ominous squeeze.

"What is it?" shrieked Wibble.

"Whatever it is, it doesn't stand a chance," said Hopper, jumping back and forth over Benjamin and Wibble. "When I get a hold of it…"

"What's going on in there?" yelled Dot from the other side. Her voice twisted and swirled, like a ghost howling through willows on a stormy night.

Chaos, thought Benjamin. He had to do something. The terrifying creature made yet another pass, molding its body against Benjamin's front leg.

"Wibble, calm down," Benjamin commanded in a loud voice. "Hopper, get onto my back." Benjamin's tone dared either of them to disobey. Even Hopper, who didn't like to be told what to do, leaped onto Benjamin's back without a sound.

"Now run," said Benjamin. "Straight ahead. Follow the path of the tunnel."

Benjamin took off. Wibble followed. They couldn't see the end of the tunnel, but they knew which way to go. Their legs moved at a quick pace, carrying them steadily forward. But the other creature kept up. It wove itself in and out of their feet like a cat playing with a mouse before delivering its final, fatal blow.

It was only minutes before Benjamin saw a faint pink glow ahead. The dawn was breaking, providing just enough light in the forest to break the inky darkness of the tunnel.

"I see the exit!" shouted Benjamin between deep breaths of air. "Keep moving!"

The light grew larger as they approached the end of the tunnel, but the creature grew more determined to stop them. Rather than traveling alongside them, it slid around their front legs, tripping them every few steps.

"Ignore it!" yelled Benjamin over his shell. "Don't stop!" They were almost to the exit. Brief gusts of fresh air mixed with the overbearing odor of the damp tunnel.

"I see it!" yelled Hopper. "I see the creature."

The mysterious beast circled them more quickly. It seemed to know that they were close to escaping and had no intention of letting them get away. Benjamin stared into the shallow water as he ran, trying to get a look at it.

He saw a flash of white. Then another and another. It zipped around them in rapid circles. They were mere steps from the exit. He could make out Dot's form standing at the other end.

"Move!" he hollered. Dot scurried away from the entrance, making room for their exit from the dark tunnel of the white beast.

Suddenly it rose out of the water in front of Benjamin. In the dim light, he saw the flash of sharp fangs. Evil, beady eyes glowed above the horrifying teeth.

Benjamin dove for the entrance. And then the creature struck.

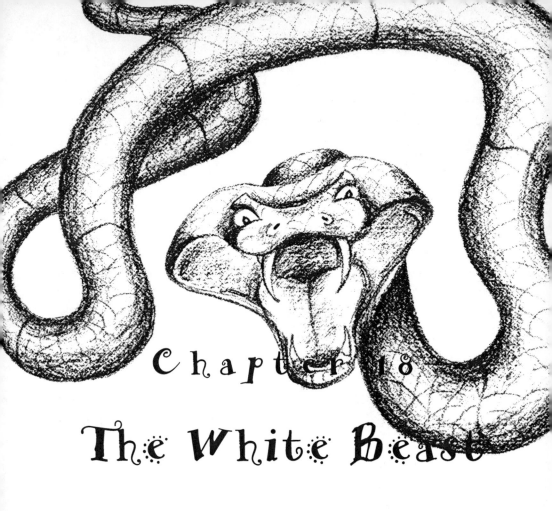

Chapter 18

The White Beast

Just as the great beast's teeth struck Benjamin's back, the group burst from the tunnel into the forest beyond. Hopper flew through the air, landing in front of Dot.

Wibble yelled, "A snake! It's a snake!"

A white snake? Benjamin thought. He'd never seen a white snake before.

The snake pulled back, then struck again, this time

through the air toward Hopper. A deformed shell dashed between the two, and the snake's teeth again landed square on a turtle shell.

"Kip?" said Benjamin, surprised.

The snake pulled itself up and fell to the ground, dazed. It shook its head a single time, then dove around Kip in hot pursuit of Hopper.

"It's after Hopper!" yelled Dot.

Hopper jumped in long arcs over the four turtles. The snake wove in and out, its fangs drawn and its red eyes burning. Kip and Benjamin watched its path, quickly learning the patterns it drew in the grass. If it had been a brown snake, or even a green snake, Hopper was certain to have become dinner. But a white snake against the dark ground was easy to track. Kip pulled back one foot and, CLUMP, stopped the snake under his foot.

Benjamin ran over and put both of his front legs on top of the snake, farther back. Its strong body writhed and struggled under the feet of the turtles.

Hopper landed on the ground in front of the snake. "Couldn't catch me, huh?" he taunted. "Not quick enough for me, huh?"

Just then a dark shadow blocked the light from the rising sun. Everyone on the ground stopped and looked up.

"A hawk," whispered Dot.

While the turtles were looking up, the snake wriggled itself free. The hawk dove.

"Hopper!" yelled Benjamin, diving between Hopper and the hawk. But the hawk wasn't aiming for Hopper. It was aiming past him.

Benjamin imagined the scene from the hawk's point of view: the dark ground of the forest, littered with brown leaves, and green weeds…four dark green turtles, a green frog…and a bright white snake slithering away.

"It wants the snake!" shouted Benjamin.

The snake stopped and looked toward the sky, its red eyes alive with terror. It darted back and forth, desperately trying to escape the hawk.

"Serves it right," said Hopper.

Benjamin suddenly felt sorry for the snake. It hadn't been evil when it tried to catch Hopper, any more than the hawk was being cruel for chasing the snake. They both had to eat.

Wibble tucked his head under his shell. Benjamin didn't blame him. This wasn't going to be a pretty sight. But almost as quickly as Wibble's head disappeared, it reappeared. Clutched in his jaw was the new shiner Benjamin had taken from Emlee's picnic. Wibble flipped it quickly around so that the shiny side faced the rising sun. Just seconds before the hawk reached the snake, a blinding reflection shot from the shiner and caught the hawk in the eye. It squawked, turning away from the shiner in mid-swoop. The snake scooted away, tucking itself under a rock near the entrance to the tunnel.

"Wow," said Benjamin. "That was brilliant."

Wibble smiled.

The snake peeked out from under the rock and collapsed into tears. It took great, gasping breaths between sobs. "I can't ever come out of that tunnel. Something always spots me," it whined. "Sure, a black snake could come out. A brown snake could come out. Even a tan snake could come out." It dropped its head onto the ground and howled. Its red eyes glowed in the light of the new morning.

"Well, I think you're beautiful," said Dot.

The snake's tears slowed. "Do you really think so?"

"Of course I do," said Dot. "But only if you promise not to eat our friend. That sort of thing could make you look terribly ugly to me."

"Just try to eat me," said Hopper. "I'll smack you on the nose if you try anything." Hopper raised one small, froggy hand.

"OK, OK," said the snake. "Besides, I could never hurt one of *his* friends." The snake pointed his snout toward Wibble. "He saved my life."

Wibble grinned. "What kind of a snake are you?" he asked. "I've never seen a snake like you in Turtle Pond."

"I'm a northern water snake," replied the snake.

"But we have lots of those," said Benjamin. "And none of them are white."

"I'm an albino," said the snake. "I was born with no color in my skin."

"Wow," said Wibble. "That's pretty cool."

"No, it's not," said the snake. "I'm different than everyone else, and I have to stay in that dark tunnel all day. Otherwise I'm nothing but a hawk snack."

The turtles looked toward the dark, musty tunnel. Wibble and Benjamin hated it in there. They couldn't imagine being stuck there all the time.

"What's your name?" asked Benjamin.

"I call myself White Snake," said the white snake.

"Creative," said Kip in a low, scratchy voice.

"Pleased to meet you, Mr. White Snake," said Benjamin. "I'm Benjamin, and these are my friends, Wibble, Dot, Kip, and Hopper."

"Pleased to meet you," said White Snake. "Listen, I don't mean to be rude, but that hawk could come back anytime."

"How about if we walk you back to your tunnel," said Benjamin. "You can hide behind us. We blend in pretty well with the grass and dirt."

White Snake smiled and nodded, and the group walked back toward the entrance to the tunnel.

"Why are your eyes red?" asked Wibble, whose curiosity always overruled courtesy.

"I don't have any color in them, either," said the snake.

"But they're red," said Benjamin.

"It's because you can see the blood vessels in the back of my eyes," he said.

"Spooky," said Wibble.

The group reached the entrance to the tunnel, and White Snake slipped into the safety of darkness. He looked out at his new friends. "Thank you again. If I can ever do anything to repay the favor…"

Benjamin looked at the dark entrance to the tunnel under Rumbler Run. Under Rumbler Run. He wondered why he hadn't thought of it before.

"The tunnel!" he yelled suddenly. Everyone jumped, even White Snake. They turned to Benjamin with questions in their eyes.

"We don't have to get the turtles over Rumbler Run," explained Benjamin. "We can get them under it."

Everyone looked back toward the creepy tunnel. It hadn't been much fun going through it, but they had all come out safely. And White Snake had been the biggest problem.

"Yes, we can lead everyone back here, and they can follow us through," said Wibble. "That is, if White Snake will promise not to eat anyone."

White Snake's red eyes lit up. "For you, Mr. Wibble, I'll do it. I'll even help you all get through," he said. "If you come during the day, there's just enough light in the tunnel for you to see me. I'll lead the turtles through the tunnel. I'll warn them about the sharpest bits of metal on the floor. I'll be waiting when you come back." He disappeared into the tunnel.

Hope blazed in Benjamin's eyes. He now knew how to save the turtles.

Dot whispered into Benjamin's ear. "The tunnel's not big enough for Jeremiah, you know."

Benjamin froze. Not big enough for Jeremiah? He studied the outside of the tunnel. Dot was right: Jeremiah would never get through there. None of the older snappers would fit. He'd have to get them across Rumbler Run.

Chapter 19

Return of the Lost Heroes

Now that the whole ordeal with White Snake was over, Benjamin greeted Dot and Kip properly.

"It's so good to see you both healthy," he said. "I was really worried."

Dot smiled. "We were pretty badly hurt for a bit," she said. "But Medi let us go the day after Wibble disappeared with Hopper. I came looking for you as soon as she let me go."

"And you went with her," Benjamin said to Kip.

Kip grumbled under his breath. "Had no choice, did I? I couldn't very well let a small turtle like her come out here on her own." He coughed, choking on the last few words.

"What's wrong with your voice?" asked Wibble.

"Landed on my throat when that rumbler got me," groaned Kip. "I haven't been able to talk right since. I'm alive though. That's what matters."

Benjamin looked at Kip. He was even more banged up than before. A big chunk of shell was missing from his right side, and his left side was dented. A long scar ran down his neck, meeting the deformity he carried on his shoulder from the first time he met a rumbler. Kip didn't seek adventure or excitement, but danger always found him. And he accepted it—no bragging, no complaining. He just dragged himself through it all. Respect for Kip rose in Benjamin. He smiled at the battered young turtle.

"It was very brave of you to go with her," said Benjamin.

Kip shrugged. "Anyone would've done it."

Benjamin knew that wasn't true. Where was Gorn? Or Roux? Nobody else had volunteered to follow Dot. Only good old Kip. And Gorn had probably given him a hard time about it.

"Let's go home," said Benjamin.

The five friends walked back toward Turtle Pond alongside Rumbler Run. They traveled much of the day, only stopping long enough for quick dips in the occasional spring along the way. Benjamin and Wibble didn't want a repeat of the previous day's scare with Hopper.

Just as the sun was starting into the western horizon, they arrived at Turtle Pond.

"It's still here," said Benjamin, his heart flooded with love for the small pond. It looked exactly as he remembered it, except that two large rumblers sat at its western shore, looming silently over the still waters.

"Will they attack?" asked Dot.

"Are there tulegs nearby?" asked Benjamin.

"No," said Kip, searching the shore for any sign of the smooth creatures.

"Then they won't move," said Benjamin. "They only move when the tulegs tell them to."

A sudden flurry of activity rose to the surface of the pond. The sentries had seen their approach, and now the whole pond knew of their arrival.

Gorn surfaced first. "Look, everyone, it's Dopey, Wimpy, Froggy, Baby, and Bumpy." He grinned, proud of his clever names. The other turtles glared at him.

King Titus crawled out of the water and frowned at Gorn. "Get back into the pond." He spoke with such authority that Gorn sunk beneath the surface.

King Titus walked over to Benjamin and his friends. "Brave heroes! We are so glad to see you all safe."

Benjamin smiled and approached the king. He bowed and then spoke in a strong voice so that everyone could hear. "Your Majesty, we bring good news. We have found a beautiful new lake…a paradise."

The other turtles murmured, and several looked sideways at Rumbler Run.

Benjamin continued. "And we have found a safe passageway there."

Cheers rose from the crowd of turtles.

King Titus raised his head. "And just in time. The rumblers arrived this morning."

"There's no time to lose," said Benjamin. "We'll leave early tomorrow. Everyone must have a good rest tonight and a big breakfast in the morning. It's a long walk to our new home."

King Titus nodded, and the crowd of turtles dove into the murky waters of the pond to prepare for the impending move. Benjamin turned to Hopper.

"Tell the other frogs. We'll bring them with us. Kip, Wibble, and Dot, make sure that all the painted turtles in the pond know." Benjamin turned toward the water.

"Where are you going?" asked Dot.

"I have to talk to Jeremiah," he said.

Dot lowered her eyes. She didn't envy Benjamin the task of delivering the news that the large snappers couldn't come on the journey to the new lake.

Benjamin swam through the murky water to Jeremiah's favorite spot. The setting sun sent streams of pink light through the depths of the pond.

"Is that you, Slider?" rumbled a deep voice.

Benjamin smiled. He'd found Jeremiah.

"Who else?" he said.

The pond shook with Jeremiah's laughter. "I guess I'm no social butterfly."

Benjamin laughed with Jeremiah. He loved the way the old snapper's bellowing chuckles vibrated through the water.

Jeremiah stopped laughing and ran his eyes over Benjamin's shell. "So, young slider, the rumbler didn't get you, then?"

Jeremiah's concern warmed Benjamin's heart. "It got me, all right, but the tulegs fixed me up."

Jeremiah's eyes widened. "The tulegs?"

Benjamin nodded. "Yes, the tulegs. Some Red tulegs took me and healed me. They weren't so bad. Are you surprised?"

The old snapper shifted in the mud. "I'm an old turtle. Nothing surprises me anymore."

"Some tulegs are good," said Benjamin. "I wouldn't have found the new lake without them."

"So you found paradise, then?" said Jeremiah.

"Yes," said Benjamin. "It's a beautiful place. And we found a tunnel under Rumbler Run."

Jeremiah raised his brow. "We?"

"Me and Dot and Hopper and Wibble and Kip."

"So the other Reds were some use after all?"

Benjamin hadn't thought about it before, but he supposed the other Reds were about as responsible for the whole plan as he was—maybe not Prince Roux, but Wibble and Kip had been a big help. And the Red tulegs too. Hopper and Dot had helped, and they weren't even Reds. Maybe Red was just a state of mind.

Jeremiah waited patiently while Benjamin finished thinking.

"Jeremiah?"

"You have something to tell me, young Benjamin?"

"Yes," said Benjamin. "It's just that…well…"

Jeremiah narrowed his eyes. "You're not going to tell me I have to talk to anyone, are you?"

Benjamin wanted to laugh, but he just couldn't. He was too worried about Jeremiah and the other big snappers.

The mischievous twinkle in Jeremiah's eyes faded. "What is it, Slider?"

"The tunnel to the new lake is too small for you and the other large snappers."

Jeremiah fell silent. Benjamin's heart was heavy.

"But I'm going to take you across Rumbler Run. All of you big snappers. Wibble and the others will lead the painted turtles and young snappers through the tunnel."

Jeremiah shook his enormous head. "No. No, young slider. The run is too dangerous."

Benjamin swam up next to Jeremiah's face. "It's not! Wibble made it across. He waited until late at night, and he and Hopper got across."

"They were lucky, that's all. The female snappers have tried crossing at all times of the day and night. Sometimes they're lucky. Sometimes they're not. I'm no spring turtle. I'm slow. I probably couldn't even get up the hill to the Run. I'll remain in the pond."

Panic rose in Benjamin's throat. His voice cracked. "But…you can't just stay here. The tulegs will order the rumblers through the pond any day."

Jeremiah smiled. "I've lived a good life here at the bottom of the pond. I think I'd just as soon end my life here too."

"I won't let you stay!" Benjamin shrieked. "You've got to try to cross the Run with me."

"And just how do you propose to make me do that?" Jeremiah's eyes met Benjamin's in a steady stare.

"Why, I'll…no, I'll…" Benjamin huffed. "I'll make the other turtles carry you up the Run."

"I'll bite them," said Jeremiah.

Benjamin threw himself against Jeremiah's shell. "I hate you! Why do you have to be so difficult?" He burst into tears.

Jeremiah stood silently in the deep muck, waiting for Benjamin to exhaust himself. At last the young turtle slid to the ground and lay in the mud next to the big snapper. Deep sobs rose from his throat.

Above the surface, night fell, and the floor of the pond grew dark. Jeremiah lifted his great neck and turned to Benjamin.

"My time has passed," he said gently. "I was once a young, strong turtle like you. My heart was full of dreams, and my head was full of grand plans. But now I'm old. You are the future. I would love to see your new lake, young slider, but that's not to be. You must go with the others. Do you hear me? You are their future as well as your own. It does nobody any good if you get killed crossing Rumbler Run with me. If you care anything for my opinion, you will tell me good-bye this very moment. You will go to the others and lead them to their new paradise. It is that thought which will give me pleasure in my last days. I will dream of you, my small Red hero, showing others the way."

He rubbed his snout against Benjamin's cheek. "It has been an honor, young slider."

Benjamin sniffled and looked into the large eyes of the old snapper. He knew he had lost. Jeremiah had made up his mind. And he had the right to do so. After all, he had been around since the days of old, when the prophecy was made. Benjamin found his voice.

"I'll never forget you," he said.

Jeremiah winked. "I know. Now go, my Benjamin."

Benjamin turned and swam away from the old snapper. After a few feet, he turned back for a final look, but it was too dark to see anymore. It didn't matter. He knew what lay in the darkness. There lay Jeremiah, the oldest and wisest turtle in the pond, stubborn and proud in equal parts. As good as dead.

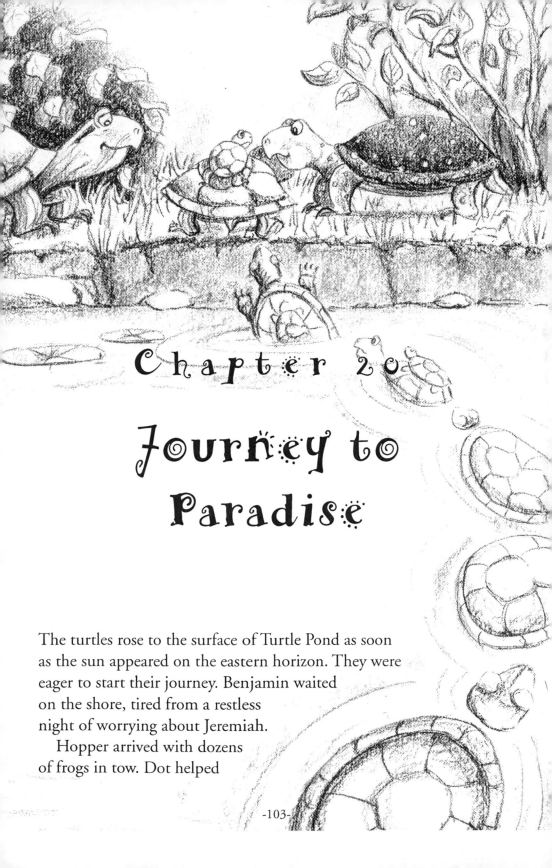

Chapter 20

Journey to Paradise

The turtles rose to the surface of Turtle Pond as soon as the sun appeared on the eastern horizon. They were eager to start their journey. Benjamin waited on the shore, tired from a restless night of worrying about Jeremiah.

Hopper arrived with dozens of frogs in tow. Dot helped

the baby turtles as they struggled onto the shore. One by one, she placed the tiny turtles onto the backs of larger turtles. She was careful not to get any of them too close to the young snappers, lest the snappers make a snack out of them.

When all the turtles and frogs had gathered, King Titus stood beside Benjamin and cleared his throat. In his most kingly voice, he made his final Turtle Pond speech.

"My dear subjects, we have had a long and happy life here in our wonderful Turtle Pond. Most of us were raised within its depths. It has given us food and safety for many years. Today we mourn the imminent loss of this lovely place and those who remain within its waters." The king took a moment to look toward the pond, his eyes flooded with sadness.

"But today we celebrate a new beginning. As the journey to a new home begins, our hearts are filled with hope for the future. For this journey, we are one family. There will be no"—the king paused to glare at Gorn—"unkind words. There will be no eaten frogs. No eaten baby turtles. All who stand here before me will make it safely to the shores of our new home. Do you all understand?"

The turtles and frogs nodded, enchanted by the majesty of their great leader.

King Titus smiled. "Good. Then today it gives me great pleasure to name a new successor to the throne. Here in Turtle Pond, the great Prince Roux"—again he paused, this time looking toward the broken prince—"was a majestic and noble leader. But a new home has different challenges. And one turtle among us has proven himself worthy of meeting those challenges. All hail our new leader, the great Benjamin."

Benjamin gulped. He sidestepped over and whispered in King Titus's ear. "But Wibble crossed Rumbler Run. And Hopper found him. And Kip and Dot found us."

The king winked. "It is you, dear Benjamin, who inspired them to action with your courage."

Benjamin wasn't sure he liked this new development, but he didn't dare question the king. "As you command," he said, bowing low on one knee.

The king raised his voice once more. "Then, my beloved subjects, turn and follow our dear Red slider, for he will lead you to your new home."

Benjamin interrupted. "You meant to say 'will lead *us*,' right?"

King Titus turned kind eyes toward Benjamin. "My dear Benjamin, I didn't name you prince of Turtle Pond. I named you king of Paradise."

Benjamin blinked, confused.

"I'm not going with you," said King Titus.

"What do you mean, you're not coming with us?" said Benjamin. The other turtles gasped.

"I am king of Turtle Pond," said King Titus. "And this is Turtle Pond. As long as some of my subjects remain, I will remain with them."

"But almost everyone is coming with us," protested Benjamin.

"The large snappers have chosen to stay," said the king. "And so have some of the old painted turtles. Don't they need a leader? Someone to give them hope? Someone to try to find them a way to escape?"

Benjamin thought of Jeremiah, sitting alone in the depths. "Yes, I guess they do. But name one of them king, and then you can come with us."

King Titus placed his forehead against Benjamin's. "They need me, young king, and I will stay with them."

"I command you to come," said Benjamin, desperation in his voice.

"You are king of Paradise. I am king of Turtle Pond. We are in Turtle Pond," said King Titus quietly. "You cannot command me." He paused. "You are their future. They need you. Now go."

Benjamin felt helpless. Did all old turtles say things like that?

Fighting the tears welling up in his eyes, he turned to the other turtles…his subjects. He gathered as much kingly composure as he could. He had watched King Titus do it dozens of times before.

"It is time to begin our journey," he said. "Follow me."

Benjamin walked slowly away from Turtle Pond. As they passed its far edge, he took one last look over his shoulder. The small, beautiful pond reflected the orange glow of the morning sun. King Titus stood by its shore, head held high, watching his former subjects depart. Somewhere in the depths, Jeremiah and the other large snappers sat in the muck, waiting for the tulegs to arrive.

Wibble, Dot, Kip, and Hopper moved up and walked with Benjamin. Their presence made him feel stronger. He shook the tear off his cheek and set his eyes on the distant forest. "To our new home," he said.

"To our new home," echoed Wibble.

The journey was uneventful. White Snake kept his promise and helped them all through the long tunnel that evening. They spent the night near the small spring in which Wibble, Benjamin, and Hopper had played. The larger turtles made a circle around the frogs and smaller turtles, protecting them from nighttime predators. But nothing came.

The next day they took the long walk along Wibble's shiner trail. When darkness fell, the sweet smell of pine told Benjamin they were close. They spent the night in dense bushes, trying to keep the excited baby turtles from giving away their hiding place with their giggles and squeals.

Benjamin paced all night, thinking about those left behind and hoping that his subjects would like their new home. *Is this what leadership is like?* he wondered. *Always worrying?*

Morning arrived at last, and anticipation buzzed around the heads of the turtles and frogs. Everyone knew they would reach the new lake that day. Benjamin was the only one who had seen their future home, and the baby turtles asked him many questions. *Is it big? Are the lily pads soft? Are the dragonflies blue?* Even Dot and Wibble couldn't help but ask.

Benjamin took his place at the front of the long parade. They were now past Wibble's shiner trail, and the rest of the trip would depend on his memory of the forest. He walked slowly, sniffing to find clues. Following his nose, he led them through the woods, past the tall weeds, and into the opening around the new lake.

Behind him Benjamin heard gasps.

"It's beautiful," whispered Dot.

"Perfect," said Wibble.

Hopper leaped over Benjamin's head and landed on the shore. "You're a genius, Benjamin. It's absolutely magnificent!"

Benjamin smiled. The others gathered round, their eyes wide with the sight of their new home.

"All hail King Benjamin!" said Medi.

The sentries of the court lifted him onto their backs and rode him around as the turtles leaped into the water, cheering. Roux plucked a daisy with his mouth and grinned.

Kip stood by the shore alone, staring across the surface of the new lake. Sparkles of sunlight danced on the water. Benjamin asked the sentries to put him down. He walked over and stood by Kip.

"So what do you think?" asked Benjamin, studying Kip's scarred face.

Kip smiled with his crooked mouth. "Paradise," he said.

Benjamin smiled back. "Yeah."

They stood together in silence, admiring the beauty of their new home.

Chapter 21

An Old Turtle's Tale

Bits of algae hung from the back of the old turtle. He cleared his throat before continuing.

"Now where was I?"

"The part where the turtles went to Paradise Lake."

The old turtle smiled at the young spotted turtle. "That's right. So they went to the new lake and lived happily ever after."

"And that was a long time ago, right?"

The old turtle rolled his eyes. *They always have the same questions.* "Yes. It was before you were born."

"Come on, tell us more," begged a small painted turtle.

Just then an adolescent turtle zipped into the group, panting. "Quick, the tulegs are here!"

The young turtles scattered, leaving behind a cloud of unsettled muck from the floor of the lake.

The dirty haze cleared, and the old turtle found himself nearly alone. All that remained was one tiny girl turtle.

"So that's how most of the turtles got here?"

The old turtle shifted in the muck. "That's right." *Another boring question.*

"Through a long, thin tunnel?"

"Yes."

She furrowed her brow. "How did you get here?"

The old turtle chuckled. *A new question at last.*

"Are you a slider?" he asked.

"How did you know?" she asked.

"Lucky guess."

She moved closer to the old turtle. He cleared his throat before he spoke.

"The tulegs are here. Aren't you going to swim away?"

"No," she said. "Before I go, I want to know how you got here."

"I told you. The turtles came through the tunnel."

She pointed one foot at the old turtle. "You're too big to go through a thin tunnel."

The old turtle narrowed his eyes. "You shouldn't get so close. You know that snappers sometimes eat young turtles."

"C'mon, Jeremiah, I mean it."

Jeremiah's eyes teased. "The tulegs came."

"And they destroyed Turtle Pond, right?"

The corners of his mouth fell. "Yes, they did. They pushed all the mud from the bottom of the pond into a big mound. We were shoved into the deep soil." Jeremiah shuddered. "The smaller turtles would not have survived."

"But you survived."

"Yes, I did. And so did some of the other turtles who stayed behind…those who were lucky enough to land on top of the dirt pile. The tulegs saw us lying there and climbed down from their rumblers. They used their strange language to call for others. Before long more tulegs came. Two had red fur…a big one and a little one. They brought big enclosures and webs."

The tiny slider swam back and forth, excited.

"And then? And then?"

Jeremiah shifted, and big sucking sounds belched forth from the floor of the lake.

"They gathered all the survivors, putting us into the big enclosures. I almost snapped at them, but then I remembered what King Benjamin said about the Red tulegs that helped him. I told the others to cooperate."

The little turtle did a backflip in the water. "So they saved you?"

Jeremiah nodded. "Yes. Those that were badly hurt were taken away by four tulegs in green wraps. We never saw them again. The Red tulegs brought the least injured of us here, to Paradise Lake."

The girl turtle cheered.

"One more question, Mr. Jeremiah. Please?"

Jeremiah grumbled. "Don't you know you're supposed to leave old snappers alone?"

"Just one. Please?"

Jeremiah stared at her. He didn't say no, so she asked.

"Who started the prophecy? You know, the one about the Reds? The one that made us find the lake?"

Jeremiah's eyes twinkled. "If you don't hurry, you're going to miss Horatio and Cleo."

"I don't care," said the girl turtle. "They'll save me a berry—I'm sure of it. I want to know. What was the name of the snapper of old who first told the prophecy of the Reds?"

A strong voice boomed from behind the small turtle. "Come on now, Agea. Emlee, Cleo, and Horatio are at the shore with berries. They're looking for you."

"Oh, all right," said the tiny turtle. "I'm going." She swam off to visit the tulegs and their pets.

A large turtle glided into the space she had occupied in front of Jeremiah. His voice was deep and clear, his demeanor confident. Behind his eye was a bright band of red.

"That you, Slider?" grumbled Jeremiah.

"Who else?" he answered.

"Well, I am a social butterfly, after all," said Jeremiah.

"I've noticed that," said the large turtle. "Whenever the children aren't here, Titus is."

Jeremiah's hearty laugh rattled the water. "Well, there's always room for you, Your Highness."

Benjamin swam over and stood directly in front of Jeremiah. "She had a good question, didn't she?"

"She's going to cause me trouble, that one. Part of your latest clutch?"

Benjamin's eyes glowed with pride. "Sure is. Princess Agea. So what *was* the name of the old snapper who made the prophecy of the Reds?" he asked.

"What's that?" said Jeremiah. "Hard of hearing these days."

"You heard me," said Benjamin.

Jeremiah's eyes burned with mischief. "Just some old snapper who wanted to light a fire under a hero."

Benjamin studied Jeremiah's face. "Then why a Red? Why not a Red slider?"

Jeremiah winked. "Didn't want to make it too easy."

Benjamin laughed. "Are prophecies supposed to be hard to figure out?"

"The ones that work are. The prophecy was fulfilled, wasn't it?"

Benjamin nodded. "More like self-fulfilled. When someone believes in a prophecy, it will come true."

"Never doubted it," said Jeremiah.

Benjamin smiled. "Strawberry or blueberry?"

Jeremiah ran his giant tongue over his beaked upper lip. "No baby turtles on the menu today?"

Benjamin lifted his kingly brow.

"Strawberry," said Jeremiah.

"Got it," said Benjamin. "One strawberry for the old prophet."

The whole lake shook with Jeremiah's laughter as King Benjamin swam toward the shore.

Paradise, Benjamin thought. *Just as it should be.*

978-0-595-39840-9
0-595-39840-5

Printed in the United States
210277BV00002B/244-765/A

9 780595 398409